Against The Odds

Robyn C Rye

Published by robyncrye, 2023.

Also by Robyn C Rye

Farnsworth Sisters
Marrying a Rogue
Rescuing Hannah

The Buckingham Sisters
Lady Maggie's Challenge
Layla's Unwanted Husband

The Evans Family
Sometimes Love is not Enough
Still the One
Moving Forward

Standalone
One More Chance
Lady Jayne's Reputation
Third Time's the Charm
Can't Stop Loving You

The Marriage Scam
An Unlikely Match
Searching For You
The Unexpected Suitor
The Lady and the Duke
Starting Over
An Unforgettable Stranger
The Duke's Revenge
The Temporary Wife
Against The Odds
Betrayed
No Good Turn Goes Unpunished
Lady Eloise's Soldier
Lillian's Forbidden Beau
Remember Me
Always Second Best
When One Door Closes
Coming Home to You
Chasing Shadows
Fool Me Once
Deserting Lady Audrey
My Unlikely Saviour
Lies and Deception
A New Beginning
Julia's Second Chance
The Hidden Enemy
The Maiden's Redemption
Miss Elizabeth's Season

Table of Contents

Copyright © 2023 by Robyn C Rye

Author's Message

As a reader, you may wonder why some words seem misspelt, but as an Australian writer, I use English spellings rather than American ones. So, NO! I am not a poor speller, and I have used the spell check, but with an Australian slant.

I loved recounting the story of Melissa and Zach, and I hope you enjoyed the unfolding story of the trials and successes they endured.

If you enjoyed the book and have a moment to spare, I would appreciate a brief review on the page or site where you purchased it. Your help in spreading the word is appreciated. Reviews from readers like you make a massive difference in helping new readers find stories like *Against the Odds.*

CONTACT ME AT
Robyncrye.author@gmail.com

Chapter 1

Melissa moved quickly through the corridors as she neared the examining rooms. Pushing through the plastic doors, she studied the patients crammed into the ER. People sat in rows, their faces wearing expressions of frustration and pain. As Melissa scanned the area, it was clear that some patients required urgent medical attention, while others presented with conditions better treated in the clinic. People presented at the emergency rooms with simple conditions that a GP could treat, and often became agitated when the staff treated others before them. Still, many others arrived in severe condition or with illnesses, and the staff triaged the patients, treating the sickest first.

As a nurse practitioner, Melissa helped care for less severely injured patients in the ER, thereby clearing the floor quickly and allowing doctors to focus on the very ill or critically injured patients. Sometimes, Melissa spent her entire shift in the ER, and when the situation wasn't urgent, she spent time in the hospital's clinic. Today was a monumental day for her as this shift was her final requirement for her diploma. There were days when she thought she would never complete her course, days when she was so tired that her brain ached, but there was a sense of satisfaction amidst all the trials. When she walked from the hospital today, sadness would tinge the excitement of returning home to begin her married life with James.

Initially, when the university accepted Melissa, she briefly considered declining the offer and remaining in Fleetwood with her long-time boyfriend. Still, James encouraged her to take up the offer and promised he would wait. They managed a long-distance relationship over the last four years with few problems. The four-hour trip between Fleetwood and the hospital at Maccy was doable on long weekends and holidays. James sometimes took a few days' sick leave, and they spent an idyllic week together, even though she had to work. It had been so long since she had seen James, and his inability to be at her graduation hurt, but he promised they would have their celebration when she returned.

Even though Melissa looked forward to the graduation celebration, she was more excited, wondering when James would propose. The last time he visited was six months ago, and during that visit, he discussed the plans for their wedding. Melissa understood that his wealthy family, prominent in the community, would bring more guests than she wanted, but she could compromise on the guest list if she could organise most of the other details. When she laughed at James during his last visit, she said planning their wedding was premature when he hadn't proposed. James assured her that when the time was right, he would make the most romantic proposal ever.

As the afternoon dragged on, Melissa found herself checking her watch. Would her shift never end? She treated many patients, most of whose conditions could be treated with over-the-counter medication. Once the ER was almost empty, Melissa walked back to her locker to pack up the medical equipment she intended to take, then started a round of goodbyes. Some colleagues were casual with their farewells, but a few of her closest friends hugged her and shed tears at the thought of her imminent departure. Melissa hoped to forge strong bonds when she started working at the Fleetwood Community Hospital.

Excitement welled as she made her way to her tiny flat, and Melissa felt giddy with anticipation. Today was the last day she would make the trip from the hospital to her flat, but the need to navigate traffic snarls settled her somewhat. Melissa parked in the residents' car park and walked toward her apartment. The block of flats housed an assortment of students and medical staff attached to the hospital, and as soon as Melissa handed in her keys, another person with dreams and aspirations would take her place. Melissa scanned her empty apartment for the last time. Over the last few days, she packed her non-essentials and sent them home via courier. With a couple of changes of clothes, her toiletries and knick-knacks packed in a small suitcase, Melissa closed the door on her life in Maccy for the last time. Tomorrow, she would be home with her family and her soon-to-be fiancé. Melissa would spend her last night in town at a motel and start early the next day. While eager to get on the road, she had promised her dad that she wouldn't set out for home after a long shift and intended to keep her word.

Even though she was tired from her long day, Melissa found it hard to sleep in unfamiliar surroundings. She had chosen a motel just off the freeway to get away during the lull before the rush hour in the morning. The flaw in her plan soon became evident as the traffic continued to drone on throughout the night. A fleet of trucks sped past, engaging their air brakes as the road's gradient changed, and sleeping here was a lost cause. After tossing and turning for hours, Melissa finally slipped into a restless sleep, only to be woken too soon by her alarm.

Still sleepy after her restless night, Melissa looked for an off-ramp along the freeway. When she finally spied a sign for a cafe with coffee and a breakfast menu, she slid across the lanes and exited the highway. The smell of food cooking drew Melissa towards a small building nestled against a rocky outcrop. The décor was outdated, but she surmised that the food must be edible by the number of customers already settled at the tables and booths. A friendly middle-aged woman smiled as Melissa approached the counter. With her breakfast ordered, Melissa slipped into an empty cubicle and inhaled the contents of the coffee cup she held in her hand.

Melissa looked around the shop as she enjoyed her meal. The patrons appeared to be mostly regulars, as the server knew most of them by name. What must it be like to work in a place where you know your customers' names? Melissa guessed she would soon find out what it was like to know her customers because Fleetwood wasn't a big town, and she thought she might bump into people she knew now and then. After finishing her breakfast, Melissa thought about texting James and her parents. But since she was a day early, she decided to surprise them both, including her fiancé. Feeling ready, Melissa put a water bottle in the drink holder and headed off for Fleetwood.

Although the trip wasn't long in terms of road miles, Melissa stopped for a walk around and a toilet break after two hours of driving. Her concentration started to slip as she neared Fleetwood, due to her long shift and a restless night. Not wanting to arrive sweaty and dishevelled, she pulled into the service station on the outskirts of town. Melissa was eager to surprise her parents and James. After a quick visit to the ladies' room to change her clothes and refill her water bottle, she continued with her journey. She was ready to surprise her parents and James.

Melissa beamed as she cruised through the familiar streets. After four years, this was where she had intended to work and live; if God willed it, she would raise her children here in this small town. Melissa decided to call on her parents first; they would be upset if somebody else told them she was in town. But when she pulled into the driveway of her childhood home, it was clear that nobody was home. She chuckled to herself. The problem with surprising people was that they didn't stay home to greet you because they didn't know you were coming. Oh well, she'd catch up with her parents later. She hoped James was home, or this surprise would fail. James lived in an enormous mansion with his parents in the most exclusive part of town. Despite growing up in the lap of luxury, James never put on airs or talked down to people. Since primary school, the two had been friends, and given their long friendship, they had never had a serious falling-out.

When puberty hit, Melissa began to see James as a man and realised she wanted more than friendship from her friend. She knew he wanted more when she caught James looking at her differently.

Melissa and James went effortlessly from friendship into a romantic relationship. The streets around James' parents' house usually lacked cars because residents parked in their garages or driveways, but today, cars lined the streets. Damn, just my luck, thought Melissa. His parents were holding a party, and if she wanted to see James, she would have to run the gauntlet of disapproval when Mrs Cartwright saw her clothes. The guests at this party were bound to have dressed to the nines, and Melissa's simple sundress and sandals wouldn't make the grade. What to do? But now that she had made it this far, Melissa decided to try to grab James before his mother realised she was there. Maybe they could slip away without anyone noticing.

Melissa drove into the adjoining street and parked her car. As she trekked back towards the house, she recognised some vehicles parked at intervals. Melissa felt a little peeved that James' parents invited their friends but not her. Did James think she couldn't get away a day early? Couldn't he at least check with her before making assumptions? Melissa's good mood dimmed as she walked towards the entrance. Once she and James were alone, she would quiz him about the party he had invited most of their friends to, but he did not include her.

When Melissa entered the room, the size of the function surprised her. Mrs Cartwright had excelled herself; this must be the most enormous function the woman had held. As Melissa dodged through groups of people, they stared and began whispering. Melissa didn't know what the weird vibe was about, but the sooner she found James, the better. Looking around the room, ignoring the smirks and whispers, she spied James among the guests at the back. She strode through the crowd with a relieved sigh until she stood before James. A bottle-blonde, rake-thin woman clung to his arm. James' expression when he saw her was not the look of adoration one should give their girlfriend after a long absence. Melissa waited for the shocked look on her boyfriend's face to disappear, but his look of surprise changed to guilt. What the hell was going on, Melissa thought.

"Hello, James. I thought I would surprise you, but the surprise is all mine. What is going on here? Who is that woman hanging all over you?"

It appeared as though James could not answer, so the woman held up her hand to show Melissa the enormous engagement ring she wore.

"We are having our engagement party, and I don't believe we invited you."

Melissa swayed on her feet, her face pale with shock. Her shaking hand went to her throat as she tried to gain composure. In a thready whisper, she said,

"Your engagement? James, how could you do this? I thought that was supposed to be my ring. You spent the last holiday with me planning our wedding, and I came home to find it all a cruel hoax. Why would you do that? How long have you been dating this woman?"

James found his voice at last.

"We've been dating for about nine months, but babe, it isn't what it seems. We need to talk later."

Melissa stepped back. Anger infused her voice.

"Nine months? You've been with that plastic woman for nine months, and in that time, you continued to sleep with me and date me? We should have talked a long time ago, not later. Answer me this: Is your engagement with that woman real?"

When James didn't answer, the woman beside him said, "Of course, the engagement is real. Are you stupid? Why would we hold an engagement party if this were a charade?" Melissa lifted her chin in defiance and said, "Then, James, I don't believe we have anything to discuss."

James looked miserable, but Melissa could not sympathise with her former beau. How could he do this to her? The party-goers were riveted to their spots by the unfolding drama. Melissa swung around to look at the crowd watching on.

"I thought some of you were my friends. Not one of you people thought to tell me that James was cheating on me? Are you such pathetic social climbers that you were afraid to offend Mrs Cartwright? Sadly, it seems that you were only my friends because you thought I'd be Mrs Carwight Junior." Melissa let out a laugh.

"If you're so interested in ingratiating yourself with Mrs Cartwright, I challenge you to be friends with the new chick. She appears to have never had an original thought in her life; your conversations with her should be riveting. Maybe she can tell you where she got her boob job done and who she gets to give her the Botox injections."

An outraged shriek sounded from behind Melissa. Swinging back around, Melissa plastered a smile on her face.

"Sorry, honey, did I give away your secrets? Never mind, these people don't care who you are or what you look like; they want to be near you when you splash money around."

Stalking towards the man who had betrayed her, Melissa said,

"James, don't bother with your pathetic excuse that this is not what it seems. If that is the case, take the damn ring off Barbie there and give it to me. No/? I thought not. This engagement party and your fiancé are exactly what they appear to be. What happened to the honest, truthful boy I loved? You're nothing but a liar and a cheat."

Melissa glared at the woman James had made his fiancée.

"By the way, honey, if he would cheat on me, someone he has known for twenty-five years, it will only be a matter of time before he cheats on you. You're welcome to him and his battle-axe of a mother. Congratulations, James, whatever convinced you to marry the plastic lady, I hope it was worth it."

With her head held high, Melissa stalked from the room. She would not let these people see her distress. Once she left the room, the conversation bubbled over. Some people had the decency to look embarrassed, but most discussed the incident as though it were the most entertaining sight of the year. James' new fiancé tittered.

"Well, that was entertaining."

James glared at his fiancée. "I just broke Melissa's heart, and you think it was entertaining? You are an unfeeling bitch, and this marriage had better bring the results promised to me. And right now, I can't stomach looking at you. Go and gossip with your bitchy friends. I'm not giving up everything I wanted for no reward."

Chapter 2

Melissa held her head high as she exited the party; no one would see her tears. When Melissa reached her car, her hands shook, and her breath came in short gasps. The life she had planned was now a crumbled ruin. She struggled to keep her fingers still enough to unlock the car door, and the tears that ran down her face made the task more difficult. Once she managed to open the door, Melissa sat in the car, staring out of the windscreen. Not only had she lost her best friend and boyfriend, but she had also lost her childhood friends. How could James blindside her like this? Didn't he have any affection for her after years of being together? Did he think the news would not reach her after she arrived in town? The only thing worse than arriving at his engagement party would be people smirking and laughing as she set up her life in the city, oblivious to James's betrayal. Inside, the guests would be gossiping and sniggering at the spectacle she had made of herself at the party. How could she have thought those people were her friends when not one person had given her a warning that James was cheating on her?

Melissa's first instinct was to go home to her parents and let them comfort her, but since she had decided to surprise everyone, her parents weren't home. Without a plan, Melissa started her car and headed toward the outskirts of town. A rest area six kilometres from the town centre looked as good a place as any to take refuge. Once she pulled over, her tears came in a torrent. Sobs tore at her throat, and Melissa bolted from the car, emptying the contents of her stomach in the bush surrounding the parking spot. Even when she thought nothing was left to expel, her tummy continued to convulse, and Melissa could do little more than slump on the asphalt until the convulsions ceased. The gravel pressed into her bare legs, but Melissa couldn't find the energy to move. There was no one in town she could talk to, so rising from the ground seemed like a waste of energy.

Melissa didn't know how long she had sat on the ground, but finally rose and staggered back to the car. Melissa wondered if her parents were home yet. After rinsing her mouth, she pulled some moist wipes from the container in the glove box and cleaned her face. She refused to let the locals see her in a total mess and didn't want to scare her parents. Even though tears continued to trickle down her face, Melissa felt more like herself and was able to face her parents. On her slow drive back into town, she tried to determine what had gone wrong between James and herself. How could the guy be planning their wedding six months ago and date another woman simultaneously? The questions without answers plagued her during her trip, but she needed to talk to her parents to help make sense of this mess.

Melissa stared at her parents' empty driveway. Where the heck were they? As she sat trying to decide her next move, she vowed never to surprise anyone again. With a sigh, she unpacked her car and grabbed something from the fridge to eat. It had been a long day, and it was only early afternoon. Who could she talk to if her parents didn't return home until the next day? Once Melissa unlocked the door, she lugged her last possessions into the house and her bedroom. With her head cocked to one side, she scrutinised her room to discover what made the place seem unfamiliar. She shook her head and headed for the kitchen, but the feeling of something strange hit her as she entered the room. What was happening to her brain, looking for problems when none existed?

A check of the fridge revealed the remains of a pasta dish. There wasn't enough food to feed both parents, so Melissa concluded that her mother had made too much and placed the leftovers in the fridge. The microwave's beep warned Melissa that her food was ready, and she transferred the remains to a plate. Seated at the kitchen table, she ate automatically, her thoughts once again on the fiasco that had unfolded this afternoon.

With nothing better to do, Melissa showered and dressed. Her sundress, meant to meet with James' approval, was not what she wanted to wear now. Dressed in jeans and a shirt, Melissa decided to call in at her favourite drinking spot and have a few drinks, but her plan was thwarted when she recognised some of the vehicles parked in the lot. She should have realised that their go-to pub, called Settlers, would fill with people wanting to discuss the debacle at this afternoon's party. Melissa was thankful that most people drove the same car year after year, so she recognised them. God help her if she had walked into the pub without being forewarned. But the presence of people she thought of as friends made her drive past the pub; where to now? The only other place that served alcohol was Trader Joe's, a rather rough place that catered to the local tradies and rougher elements. Was she up for going there for a few drinks? Sure, she was. What more could go wrong after her day from hell?

The pub wasn't busy at this early hour, but Melissa guessed the place would fill up closer to closing; she intended to leave before then. She chose a spot at the end of the bar that hugged the wall; if anyone decided to hassle her, she only had to worry about one side. The patrons already at the pub smirked when Melissa walked into the room, and since sitting at the bar, she had given four blokes their marching orders. When a bearded man sat next to her, she sighed. To her surprise, the man neither spoke nor looked at her, and they drank in companionable silence. Despite her inebriation, Melissa felt comforted by the big stranger's proximity. His body heat enveloped her, and his citrusy aroma filled her senses. Even in close quarters, he didn't crowd her.

The wine Melissa had begun her drinking spree with hadn't had the desired effect; she was drinking to forget, and if she could still remember every painful moment of her confrontation with James, then the alcohol wasn't doing its job. She waved the bartender over and switched drinks; rum and cola should help. The stranger sitting beside her looked at her glass and then at her face.

"Might be wise to call it a night, sweetheart."

"Mind your own damn business, mate. I don't need a man telling me what to do, pack of cheats and liars you are."

The man shrugged and glanced down at his drink. When Melissa called for another glass of rum, the man said, "Do you want to talk about it?"

"Why? So you can laugh at me, too?" She raised her hand for the bartender, but he shook his head.

"Sorry, no can do. If the coppers arrive and find I'm
serving a drunk woman, I could lose my license. Time for you to call it a night."

Her drinking companion said, "Did you drive here?"

Melissa found it hard to remember.

"Ah, I'm not sure. Yes, yes, I must have. I'll go home now."

When she fished out her keys, a large hand grasped her fingers and gripped them.

"No driving for you tonight. Come on, and I'll drive you home."

Raised voices registered in Melissa's mind, but what the argument was about, she didn't know. She didn't want to stand here while the blokes in the pub argued about something, so she tugged the stranger's arm. Melissa staggered a little as she rose; suddenly, she didn't feel well. The stranger grasped her arm and steered her towards the door. Panic at being at the mercy of this man surged, and she struggled to release her arm. He didn't loosen his grip, steering her towards a beaten-up truck. Without remembering how it happened, Melissa found herself inside the old beater, her seat belt snug around her. The rest of the night was a blur; the last thing she remembered was someone carrying her, and nothing after that.

Chapter 3

The morning light made Melissa want to curl up in the blanket and cover her face. She wasn't in her bed; the blankets were rough and didn't smell of the fabric freshener her mother used. Where was she? Snippets of last night filtered through her tired brain, and she opened her eyes. The large man from last night was asleep in a chair, his body in one seat and his feet perched on a nearby bench. When she tried to sit up, the pounding in her head made her groan loudly. The man rolled his feet from the counter and turned to look at her.

"How do you feel?"

"Like death warmed up. Who are you, and where am I? Did you take advantage of me last night?"

"I'm Zach Hunter, and you are at my garage. Let me get you some painkillers, and then we can do the twenty questions."

"Why am I here? I should be at home."

Zach handed her two tablets still in their blister pack and, in a gruff voice, said, "Well, that's something we agree on. I didn't go out last night intending to babysit someone, but here you are."

Melissa slipped the tablets into her mouth and drank the water Zach handed her.

"You didn't answer my question. Did you take advantage of me?"

Zach snorted. "Unconscious broads do not turn me on. When I hook up with a woman, I want her to be wholly conscious, and it has to be consensual. You failed both of those requirements last night. The bathroom is over there; clean up, and I'll take you back to your car."

Melissa gingerly lifted herself from the uncomfortable couch and entered the bathroom. The room was primitive, and she sincerely doubted that she could clean up here, considering its state. How could a man live in such squalor? The building looked like a good wind would knock it over, and the furniture looked like he had rescued it from the dump.

Once she left the bathroom, Zach motioned towards the couch.

"Sit there; we need to have a conversation."

Melissa watched Zach as he ran his hand through his straggly hair. Melissa was sure he would be handsome under all that hair if he cleaned up. Why would a man let his hair and beard grow so long that he looked like a hermit? He wasn't unattractive in his rough state; what would he look like if he shaved and had his hair cut?

"What's your name?"

"Melissa Anderson."

"Well, Melissa Anderson, you were damn lucky I was at the pub last night. You were so drunk you couldn't protect yourself, and if one of those other blokes had taken you home last night as they wanted, they would have taken advantage of you. Some blokes don't care about your consciousness or whether it's consensual. That's the best-case scenario. One of the blokes could have taken you home and invited his mates for a gang-bang."

Zach watched as Melissa's face paled, and he felt terrible scaring her, but the truth was that she was the prey last night.

"Promise me you won't go back there."

"Um, thank you for saving me and being honourable. I won't return there, but I was desperate for a drink last night."

Zach grunted. "I'm not honourable, babe, just fussy. Grab your bag, and we'll go."

"Let me buy you breakfast as a thank you. The diner serves good food, and I'd feel better if I could do something for you."

Judging from the scowl on his face, Melissa thought Zach would refuse her offer.

"On one condition. We need to move your car from outside the pub unless you're happy for the townsfolk to assume you spent the night in my bed."

Melissa smirked. "Little do they know you don't even have a bed. If you drop me off at my car, I'll meet you outside the diner."

A few minutes later, she met Zach at the front of the restaurant. As they entered, with all eyes turned towards them, Melissa regretted not anticipating the response she would receive after her meltdown the day before. Without making eye contact with anyone, she moved to a booth at the back of the room. The waitress, a woman she hadn't seen since high school, brought a bottle of water and two menus.

"I heard you were back in town."

Melissa eyed the woman, waiting for the snipe. When the woman said nothing more, Melissa nodded.

"I arrived yesterday."

"It didn't take you long to get over the boyfriend. But a warning: if you want a bit of rough after the smooth-talking James, you'd be better off looking elsewhere. This bloke here has a mile-long rap sheet, and I can't imagine your parents would be happy with you taking up with a murderer. Now that he's taken up residence here, we lock our doors, and the women don't go out alone at night."

Melissa sat stunned, trying to assimilate the information the woman spewed at her. She glanced at Zach, who sat without an expression on his face.

"You know what, Christine? You were always a nasty gossip in high school and haven't changed. We came in here for food, not gossip and abuse. Are you going to serve us, or should we go elsewhere?"

Christine laughed. "There is nowhere else to go but be my guest."

"My mother will welcome us and cook us a meal. Does Pat still own this place? Will she be happy to know that you are harassing the customers? Are you going to serve us, or are we leaving?"

With a scowl, Christine pulled out her order pad.

"What do you want?"

As they waited for the food, Zach and Melissa regarded each other.

"You're not scared of me?"

"I guess I should be afraid after what she said, but last night, you could have raped me and dumped my body in the bush, but you didn't, so my thoughts are you're not who she said you are. Sometimes, there are extenuating circumstances, but overlooking the facts is always more fun. My dad always says, "Never let the truth get in the way of a good story." I have to say, though, if the beard and the scraggy hair are an attempt at a disguise, it fails miserably."

Zach shrugged. "Not much point in cleaning up; I can't get a job here because of my reputation, and the garage will never be a goer."

"Hmm, I think you're right about the garage. Why would you buy a derelict building? You must have known how much time and money it would take to upgrade it."

"There's a story behind my purchase. I'll tell you another day, maybe. What had you drinking like a sailor last night?"

When the tears welled, Zach held up his hands.

"Whoa, Mel, if it's gonna cause you strife, you don't need to tell me."

Melissa took a shuddering breath. "Seeing as you rescued me, I think you deserve to know what turned me into a drunk without the sense she was born with."

Zach listened as Melissa told him of her relationship with James and the nasty surprise she received when she arrived yesterday. She told him about her parents' absence and inability to go to Settlers, the pub she favoured.

"I don't know this James bloke, but guys like him are a dime a dozen. It won't feel like it now, but you're well rid of him."

As Zach and Melissa left the café, Zach wondered whether he was the topic of the whispered conversations or whether it was Melissa they were discussing. He wondered at the sanity of her ex; she was kind, and even after a rough night, she was worth a second look. Zach watched as Melissa drove away. Her generosity in paying for his meal would stretch his scant resources, and the ease with which she dealt with him made him feel worthwhile. He still needed to keep his distance and not read more into her attitude than kindness, but Melissa intrigued him. How many women showed no fear when dealing with a criminal, and she never asked him to deny his past? Her guess that extenuating circumstances may have been spot on, but nobody except his lawyer considered them.

With his mind busy and his stomach comfortably full, Zach returned to the pile of rubbish that was his home. He looked around the building and cursed his brother. Surely, after giving Zach the okay to buy this falling-down hovel, Michael could have offered some money to help Zach make repairs. Due to Michael's laziness, he barely made ends meet and could see no way out of his mess. Zach knew that if he came across Melissa again and she pressed him, he would tell her how he ended up buying a pile of rubble. The truth, though, would cause him embarrassment, and she would think he was a fool for being taken in so effortlessly.

Chapter 4

Melissa headed toward home, her mind in a jumble. After Christine's comments at the diner, she should be wary of Zach, but she discovered she trusted him. His conduct the night before had shown that he was a man of integrity, and if she came upon him again, she would treat him with the same kindness he had shown her. His presence made her feel safe when he sat next to her at the bar the night before. What was the real story behind his conviction? Gossipers like Christine often didn't bother discovering the truth behind the rumours they spread, and didn't care that those untruths could impact another's well-being. After seeing where Zach lived and the lack of amenities at his garage, Melissa became concerned. She knew it wasn't her place to interfere, but the way he wolfed down his breakfast suggested he didn't eat regularly. Busy-body or not, Melissa decided to feed Zach whenever she could.

As the turn into her street loomed ahead, Melissa shut off thoughts of the intriguing Zach Hunter and focused on the reunion with her parents. Even though her life plans had changed, she thought settling in Fleetwood with her parents nearby would be her choice. Her four years away had given her skills she would never have developed if she had remained at home, but now she was ready to bring those skills to her small town. A fleeting thought crossed her mind: was Fleetwood the best place to live? Her friends had turned their backs on her when they knew she wouldn't be the next Mrs Cartwright. Lifelong friendships disappeared seemingly overnight, but Melissa knew what she experienced at the party had been at least nine months in the making.

Melissa pulled her car into the driveway next to Brett's vehicle. She guessed her dad's car was in the garage, and it was better to park behind him than block Brett. Melissa took a steadying breath and opened the car door. She grabbed her bag and headed for the front door. Just as she reached out to open it, the door burst open, and her dad stood there with a welcome smile. Melissa stepped into his arms for a hug, and the small show of affection set off another round of tears.

"Hey, hey, what's all this?"

"I have lots to tell you, some of it upsetting."

"Come into the kitchen, and we can grab a cuppa and talk about your upsetting news."

As they reached the kitchen, Melissa looked around. Before she could ask the question on her lips, her brother looked up from his meal and sneered.

"So, the prodigal daughter has returned. Should we slaughter the fatted pig and have a feast?"

"Brett, that's enough."

"Ah, did I interrupt something? I know I haven't been home for months, but that's what it took to get my qualifications. I feel like I'm missing something."

The rebuke from her father was welcome, but what had made Brett moody and critical? He knew she was at uni, although he never tried to visit.

"Why should I stay quiet? It's taken her long enough to show up. I would have thought that she would have come home sooner."

"What's going on? What's happened? Where's mum?"

"Melissa, I have some upsetting news. Do you want to tell us what happened to you or me to go first?"

"Dad, you're freaking me out. Tell me what the matter is."

Brett interrupted. "Don't play the innocent here; you know damn well the problem, and you're too damn tied up being a big wig in the city hospital. Couldn't you have put your skills to use here better?"

"Dad?"

"Sit, and I'll tell you, and thank you, Brett, for keeping your mouth shut about something you don't understand. Lissa, do you remember when your mum and I came to your graduation? You commented that she didn't look well, and the truth is, she wasn't well. An oncologist we saw diagnosed stage four ovarian cancer."

Melissa jumped up. "How long has she got?"

"Six months at the most."

"Why wasn't I told? I would have come home straight away."

"Darl, your mum and I knew you would leave your studies and come home, but she didn't want you to do that. She feared that if you came home to nurse her, you wouldn't pick up your studies after she was gone, and she wanted to give you a career."

Tears rolled down Melissa's cheeks.

"Damn it, would you have told me when the funeral was if I hadn't finished my course?"

Brett closed his gaping mouth. "You didn't tell her?"

John Anderson sighed. "Your mum thought she was doing the right thing. She was worried that if we told Melissa, she would defer her course and come home. I couldn't change her mind."

"Where is Mum?"

"We turned the lounge room into a bedroom for your mum. It's closer to the bathroom and bigger than our room."

Melissa turned on her heel and headed for the lounge room. When she opened the door, she was appalled. The room was dark and stuffy, and Melissa's first instinct was to throw open the curtains and open the windows, but she assumed they were like that for a reason.

"Mum?"

"Melissa, you're home. Come over here."

There was joy in her mother's voice, but her frail body and skeletal face made Melissa want to cry. While she was drinking herself silly, moaning about her lot in life, her mother struggled through hell.

"God, mum. I don't know what to say. How did this happen?"

"Maybe your dad could tell you. I get tired so quickly."

"Okay. I'll talk to Dad. Can I get you something to eat or drink?"

"I don't eat very much; food doesn't seem to agree with me these days. Could you bring me a glass of water?"

Once she returned to the kitchen, Melissa's tears rose, and her heart ached with the knowledge that her mother was close to death. Regardless of what the doctor said, Melissa guessed that her mother had at least a month or two.

"Please tell me everything that's led to mum being this ill."

John Anderson sighed. "Your mother was feeling unwell and having stomach pains. I wanted her to go to the doctor, but she said it was the wind. I came home one day, and she was on the couch, curled up, with a hot water bottle on her stomach. I insisted she make an appointment with Doctor Burns. He did some tests and couldn't find the problem, so he sent us to the hospital for blood tests and an ultrasound. The tests concluded that your mother had ovarian cancer. Doctor Burns referred her to an oncologist, Doctor Brian Nash, who diagnosed her with stage four cancer. He said it was too advanced to make treatment an option, so he sent her home and suggested I make her comfortable. Doctor Burns was to oversee your mother's palliative care, but he doesn't know what your mother needs or how to acquire things, so we've been left to our own devices. And God, Melissa, I feel like a failure. Your mother is skin and bones and in pain, and I don't know how to help her."

Melissa rose from the table and wrapped her arms around her dad. She felt him shudder as the tears he'd tried to hold back spilled out. When her dad regained his composure, Melissa got up and put the kettle on. She sorted through her father's things and fiddled with teabags and cups. No one spoke while they waited for the kettle, but when Melissa placed cups in front of her dad, Brett, and herself, she rummaged through a drawer and pulled out a pad and pen.

"We need to make a list of the things we need. The first question is, why are the curtains and windows closed?"

"Your mum says the light from the outside hurts her eyes."

"Okay, the first thing on the list is a good pair of sunglasses. We need to open up the room for fresh air."

As the three Andersons brainstormed ideas, Melissa jotted down their thoughts. When the suggestions stopped coming, Melissa added a few of her own.

"Mum needs an IV drip and stand, a wheelchair and a hospital bed that lifts and lowers. She looks too weak to get to the bathroom, so I'm guessing you carry her?"

When her dad nodded, she said, "You're no good to her if you get sick; a catheter will make your life easier. I can go to the first-aid shop in the morning, get the things I can, and get the rest from the hospital. Tomorrow, we need to see Doctor Burns for the saline drip and some morphine prescriptions. I'll let the hospital know I won't start this week, but I can do night shifts once we get organised."

Brett glared at Melissa.

"You come in at this late stage and take over. Who made you the boss?"

"It's clear to me that Dad has shouldered the bulk of Mum's care and the worry by himself. I'm here now as a daughter and a medical practitioner, and I'll do all I can to relieve Dad of some pressure. What do you want me to do? Curl up in a corner and cry? Grow up, Brett; this isn't a competition."

Chapter 5

With the dire situation at home, Melissa forgot to discuss James' betrayal until the following day at breakfast. When her dad raised the subject, sadness overwhelmed Melissa.

"Lissa, when you arrived home yesterday, you said you had news, but with the difficulties in caring for your mother, I forgot to ask what happened to make you sad."

Melissa gave a cynical laugh. "I thought it was a good idea to surprise everyone yesterday because I had left a day earlier than expected. I came here, but you weren't home, so I went to James' house."

Tears welled in Melissa's eyes. "They were having a huge party celebrating James's engagement to a blonde, wafer-thin bimbo. All my so-called friends were there, and not one of them told me James was dating another woman. They've been together for nine months."

Brett interrupted. "That can't be right. Mum and Dad went to your graduation and said that James had spent the week with you a few months before. Wasn't he supposed to propose in the most romantic way possible?"

"Yes, so it looks like he was cheating on her or me; who knows? It seems he used that romantic proposal on someone else. I'm devastated, and I've lost James, but I've also lost the friends I made in school because I'm no longer going to be Mrs Cartwright."

"Darl, I'm so sorry. The man is a fool if he thinks he has found a better woman than you. And while I'm upset for you, your story begs the question. If you arrived yesterday, where did you spend the night? Don't tell me you slept in your car?"

"No, but I guess I have to tell you the whole sordid story; you'll hear the gossiper's version sooner or later, and I'd rather you knew the truth."

Melissa related the facts from the night before, but her father stopped her when she got to the part about going home with Zach.

"You went home with some man you met at the bar?"

"Yes. I drank too much, and when the bartender wouldn't serve me any more alcohol, I decided to drive home. Zach took my keys from me and bundled me into his truck. When I woke this morning, I couldn't remember what had happened, but I was fully clothed, asleep on his couch, and he was asleep in a chair; I figured I'd had a lucky escape. I asked all the appropriate questions, and he said he likes his partners to be conscious and consenting, and I failed both of those requirements last night. As a thank you for saving me, I took him to the diner for breakfast."

Brett's brow furrowed, and he said, "What's the guy's full name?"

"Zach Hunter."

"Holy shit, that guy's a murderer. You're lucky he didn't slit your throat in the night."

"That's the second time someone has said that to me, and it's hogwash. Last night, he could have raped me, murdered me and disposed of my body, and nobody would be the wiser. I'm unsure what the murder wrap is about, but there must be extenuating circumstances. You know what this town is like; if you don't know the truth, you make it up. Even if I listened to gossip, I would discount half of what I hear."

"You're such a soft touch, sis. Don't be fooled because he did the right thing once. Please stay away from the guy; he's bad news."

"Brett, do you want the ugly truth that Zach shared with me this morning? Last night, the pub's patrons were so-called upstanding citizens, tradies and married men, your mates, and most of the blokes offered me a lift home. If I had gone home with one of those upstanding citizens, I would have woken and known that someone had taken advantage of my inebriated state. There were men there who would have taken me somewhere quiet and invited their friends to share, so don't tell me he is bad news. He showed integrity, and I'm grateful for that."

Brett muttered about stupid women as he headed for the front door. When the door slammed shut behind him, Melissa addressed her father.

"I know, Dad, what I did was foolish, but it won't ever happen again. I've learned my lesson. Now that we have hashed over last night, I'll go to mum for a few minutes before starting my shopping list of aids. Can you ring Doctor Burns and make an appointment? Is there someone who can sit with mum while we're there?"

"Peggy next door offered, but I've never taken her up on the offer. She might sit with your mum for a while."

"You might need to accept the offer of assistance from friends and neighbours. Sitting by mum's bed for weeks, which I assume you've done, is not good for your health. And someone else tending to mum gives her a little variety."

Her dad nodded. Melissa thought he looked like a drowning man going under for the third time, and she vowed to make changes to help her father survive the illness that was killing his wife.

After spending time with her mother, Melissa grabbed her list, headed to her car, and found her front tyre flat. She cursed as she unloaded the repair tools from the boot and placed them beside her wheel. Try as she might, Melissa couldn't budge the wheel nuts. While she glared at the flat tyre, her dad exited the house.

"I thought you were going shopping."

Melissa moved away from the car, and her father realised what was wrong.

"It doesn't help if you know how to change a tyre if someone uses a ratchet gun to tighten the wheel nuts."

"Let me see if I can help. We'll have to call the mobile mechanic if I'm too weak in my old age."

Much to Melissa's relief, her father managed, with some swearing, to loosen the nuts. She pulled the spare tyre out from under its cover in the boot and rolled it towards the front of the car. Melissa looked at her hands and shirt once the spare wheel was on and the flat one in the boot.

"I never manage to change a tyre without getting filthy. I'll clean up and then take the tyre to the tyre place before I start my shopping spree."

"That's a good idea; I'm not happy about you driving around without a spare. Do you need money?"

"No, I'm good for now."

When Melissa pulled up at the tyre repair place, the lack of cars in the lot cheered her. Hopefully, the bloke could fix her tyre while she waited. As she approached the counter, she recognised the man as one of the men from the pub last night. She conceded that he hadn't made any advances to her, but he had leered at her last night, and the smirk on his face this morning made her angry. Melissa pushed down the angry words she wanted to spew at the man; this was the only tyre repair business in town.

"Good morning. I have a flat and hope you can repair it this morning. I'm not driving far, but I'd prefer to have the spare available if I get another flat tyre."

"No can do, lady. I'm too busy. I might get to it in two or three days."

Melissa looked around her and noted the lack of other customers.

"What do you mean you can't fix my tyre for a few days? There's nobody even here."

The sweating, greasy man shook his head.

"Just what I said, luv. I have an eighteen-wheeler booked in; the bloke will arrive any minute. Why would I do your one lousy tyre and make an important customer wait?"

"But my tyre would only take you a few minutes. I don't want to be driving around without a spare tyre."

"Well, you've got two options: wait for me or find someone else to do it."

"Who else in town repairs tyres?"

The man smirked at her. "I believe the convict thinks he's a mechanic. You're on intimate terms with him, so I believe, so get him to fix your flat."

Melissa gaped in amazement. Whether or not Zach could fix her tyre, Melissa was never going back to that sleazy male to have him fix her car. Even if she had to drive to the next town, an hour away, she would rather do that than deal with the man. With a shake of her head, she stormed out of the tyre repair shop.

Melissa fumed as she drove across town. Wait until that fat, greasy man arrived at the hospital for treatment; she might have to give him the same stellar service he offered her. When Melissa pulled up in the driveway of Zack's garage, there was no sign of him. Damn. It looked like she might have to take a long drive. Should she walk around the back to see if he was there? A better idea popped into her head, and Melissa learned in the car window and blew the horn. She waited a moment and then repeated her action. As Melissa considered blowing the horn again, a furious man stormed out of the building and barrelled toward her. Her eyes widened as she watched him advance.

"What the hell are you doing sitting out here like lady muck and blowing the horn?"

"Ah, I didn't know how else to get your attention."

"Well, you've got it now, so you can get in your car and drive away."

"Did I interrupt something important? I'm sorry for thinking you could help me. Forgive my foolishness."

Melissa turned on her heel and strode towards her car. As her hand contacted the door handle, Zach groaned. Who would have thought drinking at the pub would cause him so much grief?

"Mel, stop. What do you need?"

Melissa swung around.

"I know your role in life is not as my guardian angel, but I have a flat tyre that the tyre place won't fix until the end of the week. Can you repair tyres? I wasn't sure, but after the guy leered at me and suggested I get you to fix the tyre, I wouldn't let him make me wait a week."

Zach sighed. "Pop the boot, and I'll get it out; it'll save you from getting dirty."

"Yeah. Dad helped me change the wheel because some idiot must have used a ratchet gun to tighten the nuts, and I couldn't get it off and had to change my clothes before going shopping."

"How long will your shopping take?"

"I'm not sure; it depends on whether the medical shop has the supplies I need."

"What are you buying at the medical supply shop? Doesn't it sell equipment and stuff?"

Tears welled in Melissa's eyes, and she swiped at them.

"My mother has stage four terminal cancer. Her doctor knows nothing about palliative care, so my dad has been doing his best, but he has no idea, either. The quack her doctor referred her to threw his hands in the air and sent her home to die. We need equipment to make her last days more comfortable, and I know some of it, like a lift chair, will be beyond our budget, but I'll get everything I can."

"Why do you need a lift chair?"

"Mum is too weak to walk to the bathroom, so she uses a wheelchair. Dad lifts her from her bed to the chair, and I'm concerned for his health if he continues to overdo things. But the chairs are costly, so we must do without one."

"That's tough. Take as long as you like. I'm not going anywhere."

Zach ran his hand through his hair, shook his head and rolled the tyre away from where Melissa stood. He thought his life was tough, but for Melissa to arrive home to find her mother dying of cancer, his problems seemed inconsequential. He wondered whether fate had brought them together in this place to help each other survive their hardships.

When Melissa collected her tyre, she handed Zach thirty dollars. He thrust the money back at her.

"I'm not a charity case. I don't need your damn money." Melissa shook her head,

"The bloke at the tyre service would have charged me thirty dollars, and he wouldn't have thought I considered paying the bill charity. Take the money, Zach. If you get your business up and running someday, will you refuse to let your customers pay?"

Zach growled. "God, woman, you are aggravating. Do you always have to argue with me?"

Melissa grinned. "Only when you're being an ass."

Chapter 6

Melissa arrived home laden with packages and boxes of equipment. When her dad came to help her bring the purchases in, Melissa suggested taking the packages into her mother's room and unloading them there. The first thing Melissa unpacked was a pair of sunglasses for her mum, and when her father fitted them to her mother's face, Melissa threw open the curtains and windows, letting in the fresh scents from the garden.

As Melissa set up the equipment and unloaded the packages, she explained their purpose to her mum and dad. She set up an air purifier and showed her mum the audiobooks she had purchased, as well as meditation and relaxation music, and a stand for the IV she intended to set up to help with hydration and pain relief.

When Peggy, their next-door neighbour, arrived, Melissa and John Anderson headed for the doctor's surgery. Melissa asked medical questions, and when the doctor deferred to her father, John Anderson asked Doctor Burns to answer Melissa's questions. Melissa was impressed with Doctor Burns; he didn't pretend he knew what equipment and medications a patient in palliative care needed, but he cared about his patient and wanted to do his best for her.

"Doctor Burns, my daughter is a nurse practitioner and has a far better understanding of her mother's needs than mine. Would you please answer her questions regarding Pam's care? Anything we can do to make this time more comfortable for her is of value."

John and Melissa left with prescriptions for saline bags and vials of painkillers for the IV. Melissa intended to visit the hospital the following day to discuss her employment and collect the prescription items.

Brett, John and Melissa sat at the table. Melissa had cooked a tuna mornay, and the men, who were not the best cooks, dug into their food enthusiastically. Melissa updated Brett on the purchases for her mother and let him know what she would do tomorrow about collecting supplies.

"We could've used your muscles this morning. Did you notice I had a flat tyre when you walked out to your car?"

"Yeah, I did, but I was running late, so I guessed the roadside assistance could take care of it for you."

"Well, gee, thanks. The roadside assistant, known as Dad, helped me out."

"Did you have any trouble getting it fixed?"

"Yeah, actually, I did. That fat, smelly guy from the tyre service said they couldn't fix my tyre until the end of the week. He leered, smirked, and suggested I get Zach to fix the tyre, so I did."

Brett scowled. "You saw that criminal again today?"

"You know something, Brett, since I've returned, a polite, conviction-free man dumped me, my squeaky-clean friends unfriended me in droves, and that bloke at the tyre service made lewd inferences and faces at me. From where I'm standing, Zach Hunter is a far better person than the people I've come across lately. And if I see him again, I will certainly make it my issue to be friendly."

"Dad, speak to her. Tell her the man is dangerous, and she should avoid him."

"I must say, Lissa, I'm a little concerned about this bloke you keep running into, but you've been away from home for four years without incident, so I will trust you, but be careful. What's on your list for tomorrow?"

"I have to go to the hospital to organise some casual work and pick up the medical supplies for mum. I feel so helpless; I know I'm making mum more comfortable, but I wish I had a miracle drug."

"Darl, we can only do so much. We can play the if game forever, but it doesn't help. A miracle cure will not pop up, so we have to deal with the hand that fate has dealt us."

"Hmm."

Something that niggled at the back of Melissa's brain crystallised into a memory.

"Holy hell, I do have a miracle cure! I can't believe it slipped my mind. Dad, do you remember a few years ago, I couldn't decide what I wanted to do as my major once I had my nursing qualifications? I spent three months working in Dr Winn's lab. He was an oncologist who was tired of watching people struggle with cancer. He developed an experimental drug that he tested on people living with cancer. The results were spectacular, but the medical board wouldn't authorise distribution of the medication until thousands of people had trialled it. He faced significant pushback from other oncologists and was unable to meet the medical board's goals. The self-interest of medical professionals outranked the benefits to their patients. They called him a quack and a fraud, using skewed statistics to discredit him, but I was there and helped collate the results. The drug did what he said it would, and the inability to make it available to the general population is a crime. Let me see if I can contact him."

Brett sneered. "You'd let some wacko use an experimental drug on mum? What if there are side effects?"

Melissa glared at her brother. "Doctor Winn is not a wacko, and what side effects could be worse than dying? Mum cannot survive this illness without a miracle cure, and Doctor Winn developed one. If the public knew what was happening with the medication, there would be riots in the street. The number of people the drug could help would change cancer from certain death to a curable disease."

John Anderson had followed Melissa's explanation without commenting. When she looked at him with an excited expression, he spoke.

"Could this work, Lissa?"

"Yes, if we haven't left it too late, Dad. Doctor Winn treated fifty people while I was at the lab. There was a three-month trial. At the end of the test, half of the participants were clear of cancer; fifteen people had lesions small enough to be operable, five had the tumours still there, but the medication had halted the growth, and five had no benefit and died. The medication helped with pain, and each trial participant reported increased appetite. Those are great odds. Please, let me find him and ask about the drug."

"Let's keep this to ourselves until you speak to the doctor. I don't want to get your mother's hopes up if it isn't a goer."

"That's a good idea. I'll see if I can contact Dr Winn tomorrow morning. I don't have a private number, but I have the number and his extension at the lab. Dad, there's something else I'd like to talk about regarding Mum's care."

"God, Melissa, anyone would think you were a great scholar capable of organising the world. Why don't you leave Dad alone? He has been coping quite well without your bossiness."

"Okay, Einstein, how many hours of sleep a night does Dad get? How many times a day do you relieve Dad to have a break from sitting with Mum and helping her? When was the last time Dad left the house to do some shopping or catch up with friends? You don't know, do you? I know you are upset about Mum's illness, but it doesn't impact you every hour of every day as it does Dad. Maybe if you helped out a little, you would understand the full impact this has on Dad."

When Melissa finished her tirade, she glared at her brother. His expression had changed from combative to sheepish.

"Sorry, my bad. What was your suggestion?"

"Dad, I can take over part of Mum's care, but we should hire one of the blue care nurses to come in two or three times a week to help Mum shower and get her out of the house. The garden at this time of year is lovely, so a short stint in the garden might perk her up a bit. We must relieve you for part of each day, and the blue nurses can help."

John Anderson nodded.

"I will admit that I feel pretty weary. I love your mother and don't want her to think I've abandoned her, but we can spread the shifts if we work out a roster. As long as someone is with her, that should work."

Melissa sighed with relief. Her mother's condition wouldn't deteriorate if she could get Doctor Winn to help, and she didn't want her father's health to fail with the stress of looking after his wife. She thought her father might fight her on this point, but having his acceptance relieved her worries.

A knock on the door roused everyone from the kitchen table. Melissa's dad returned to the sick room, and Brett headed for the lounge room. Melissa shrugged and walked towards the front door. Before she could answer, the knocking came again.

"Not impatient, much," she said as she opened the door.

Her mouth gaped open at seeing her ex-boyfriend standing in the doorway. After gathering her wits, she said,

"What the hell are you doing here? I never want to see you again, and I'm sure I made that clear."

"Melissa, I need to talk to you about our situation, but I need you to clear up a report I heard from numerous sources before I do. The reports said your car was outside Joe's bar all night, and you went home with that criminal fellow. Tell me that's not true."

"What I do or don't do is no concern of yours, and we don't have a situation to discuss. You lied to me, cheated on me, and blindsided me. You are now engaged to the type of woman you said you hated, proving that everything you ever told me was most probably false. Leave me alone, James; the hurt you inflicted will fade with time, but my faith in you will never be restored."

"Melissa, what you do reflects on me, and we need to discuss where we go from here. I have a suggestion to put to you, but first, I need you to promise you won't see the murderer fellow again."

Melissa barked out a laugh. "You missed my point. You have no control over my life, and if I want to sleep with fifteen different blokes, it is of no concern to you. I don't want to hear your suggestion; I wouldn't be interested even if you decided you had made a mistake and wanted us to resume our relationship. Get out of my house, or I will call Dad and Brett to evict you."

"You will regret not listening to me. My family has a lot of influence in Fleetwood, and you could find your life here in town more difficult."

"What? More difficult than being the laughingstock of the town? Because you can't get your way, you want to threaten me? My mother is critically ill, and I have no time or enough patience to listen to your pathetic excuses. You've made your choice, and I hope Plastic Barbie makes you happy, but I will not let you try to validate your betrayal. Go away."

John Anderson approached the door as Melissa slammed it shut."Who was that?"

"It was James wanting to talk and then issuing threats when I told him to get lost. It seems he and his influential mother can make my life difficult. What did I see in him? When did the kind, decent guy I loved vanish? I thought I knew him better than anyone else, and he has become someone I can't even recognise. After what he did to me, how can he think I want to discuss anything with him?"

"Some people want to eat their cake and have it as well. I'm sorry your friends deserted you, and I can't explain how someone you have been friends with all your life can throw you over so easily. It would be best if you stuck to your guns. You still have your family, and we'll look after you."

Chapter 7

Pam Anderson looked around the room that had become her prison. Propped up in bed, she had a better view of what was happening and could see Melissa's changes to the room. Pam had more to do during the day, shielded by sunglasses, audiobooks, and calming music, but her inability to even get to the bathroom was demeaning. She tried to stay positive, not wanting her family to know how sad and anxious she felt, but it was hard to keep up the facade.

When Melissa entered the room with a bright smile and a chirpy demeanour, Pam felt worse. Melissa had to be suffering from her broken heart, yet here she was, running errands and looking after her mother; life didn't seem fair.

"How are you feeling, mum?"

"Not too bad this morning. What are you up to today?"

"I have some errands to run and a trip to the hospital. I have to pick up some supplies and sign on to their system to organise a couple of weekly shifts. That ought to keep me current. I wondered if you wanted a television or a DVD player here so you could watch movies?"

"It seems like a lot of trouble."

"We want you to be as comfortable as possible, and if keeping your mind occupied achieves that, then that's what we'll do."

"I'll discuss it with your dad. Why don't you send him in and go and do your errands?"

As Melissa turned to leave the room, Pam said, "Melissa, you know you can talk to me about what happened between you and James? I can't offer explanations, but I can provide a shoulder to cry on."

Melissa turned to face her mother, and her shoulders dropped, the perky demeanour disappearing.

"Arriving early yesterday was the best decision I've ever made. Would James and my so-called friends have pretended that the engagement party hadn't happened if I hadn't walked in on it? I can't get my head around what happened. You know, I thought I knew James better than anyone else in the world. His engagement with the type of woman he always said he hated makes me question everything I thought I knew about him. And to make matters worse, not one of my friends thought to tell me he was dating someone else; he completely blindsided me."

"I hate to speak badly about someone I don't know well, but I'll bet his mother had a hand in his engagement to the other woman. Mrs Cartwright never thought you were good enough for him so that she may have somehow coerced him into the arrangement. I'm sorry about your friends. People show their true colours when money is involved, and their abandonment of you says more about their characters than it does about you."

After asking her father to sit with his wife, Melissa put her messages on hold while contacting Doctor Winn. She dialled his number and asked for his extension; the woman who answered asked who was calling, and shortly after, Simon Winn came on the line.

"Melissa, my dear, how are you? It's been a while since we talked."

Melissa grinned. Simon Win was one of her favourite people. He was warm and caring but irreverent and didn't suffer fools lightly.

"I have to admit to an ulterior motive other than hearing the sound of your melodic voice."

"So, you want to ask me a favour?"

"Yes, yes, I do."

"Okay, spit it out, woman, and I'll see what I can do."

Melissa's story came pouring out, and Simon Winn made encouraging noises as she continued. When she finished her narration,

Melissa said, "I would run it as you did, with blood pressure, temperature and heart rate checks. It's her only hope, and I know you took a lot of flak when you did your first trials, but if this works for Mum, we should push the information about your struggle to the media. Once people living with cancer realise there is hope, they will insist on being one of the trial participants."

The silence at the end of the phone made Melissa wonder if she had lost the connection.

"What happens if the treatment doesn't work on your mum?"

"I will know that we did everything we could to help her. Making her comfortable and watching her die is heartbreaking. If we have a go, I'll feel better doing something."

"Okay, give me your details, and I'll order a refrigerated carrier to deliver the drugs. I can pack and send the samples today, so you should receive the medication tomorrow. Please do me a favour; keep the treatment confidential until we are ready to release information to the media or crawl back under a rock.

"You have my word that the treatment will remain confidential, and you have my eternal gratitude."

Simon Winn chuckled. "You realise I might call in a favour sometime?"

"Whatever the favour, I will endeavour to fulfil my obligation."

Melissa hung up the phone; her smile told the story of her success. She felt like doing a jig. Before leaving the hospital, she stuck her head into her mother's room.

"Dad, Doctor Winn is on board. The medication will arrive tomorrow. Do you want to discuss this with mum by yourself, or do you want me to sit with you while we tell her what I've organised?"

"John, what did Melissa do? What medication?"

John Anderson chuckled. "You never could stand the suspense of not knowing what was happening. Lissa, why don't you go to the hospital, and I'll talk to your mum? Come and join us when you return, and if there are any questions I can't answer, we will get you to explain."

"Okay, I'm going now."

The excitement of convincing Simon Winn to part with his medication stayed for the drive to the hospital. The paperwork for her hospital registration took quite some time, and Melissa was frustrated with the hospital's HR department for its slow pace. When she finally exited the human resources office, Melissa took her prescriptions to the nurses' desk to have the on-duty staff fill them. As she waited, Melissa could hear shouting and thumping on the nearby room's walls. A wailing nurse ran from the room, whining and shaking.

"That man is an animal. And he can die of his injuries for all I care. When I said he had to fill out the paperwork, he started shouting and throwing the equipment on the table near him."

More loud thumps attested to the patient's state of mind. Extra nurses were collected at the desk, and everyone refused to enter the examination room. Melissa was pulled into the drama by her presence at the desk.

"I don't know why they let scum like him into the hospital; everyone knows he's a murderer, and the police let him settle in our town. God knows who he'll murder next."

Melissa's head shot up. "Can I introduce myself? I'm Melissa Anderson, your new nurse practitioner. If you get me a white coat and a stethoscope, I'll enter the room. My registration at this hospital is current; I signed the paperwork a few minutes ago."

"I can't let you go in there. I'll call one of the wardsmen, and they can throw the criminal out."

"Please, hold off with the eviction. Get me the gear I need, and I'll treat the patient."

The head nurse shook her head but handed Melissa a white coat and the stethoscope. As she put on the coat, Melissa glanced at the sobbing nurse. Melissa rolled her eyes and headed for the door of the examination room. She opened the door a fraction, and a missile hit the door.

"Good shooting, Zach, but you'd better let me in unless you want to die of old age. It's Melissa Anderson, and I need to examine your injuries."

Melissa pushed the door open and walked into the room without further ado. She quickly surveyed the mess on the floor.

"Hurling missiles will not endear you to the population of Fleetwood Hospital. The room looks like a five-year-old threw a tantrum in here. Show me what the towel around your hand and arm is hiding."

When Zach removed the towel, Melissa grimaced.

"Ouch, that looks painful. The hysterical nurse didn't say what triggered the fit of temper, so what's the go?"

"The stupid cow said I needed to complete the paperwork before the doctor would look at me. When I told her I couldn't fill in the paperwork, she gave me a spiel about hospital protocol, and when I repeated that I couldn't fill out the documents, she started to swear and shout, so I grabbed the first thing I could and threw it at the silly bitch."

"Did you consider asking her to get someone else? Throwing things at the attending nurse seems like an overreaction. Never mind. Have you had a tetanus shot in the last ten years? If you have no problem with me treating you, I'll get the documents and some pain relief."

"I didn't know you were a doctor."

"Well, we hardly swapped life stories when we first met, but I'm not a doctor; I'm a nurse practitioner. It means I can treat you if no doctor is available, and after your tantrum, nobody will put themselves out for you from the look on the hospital staff's faces. I'll be back in a minute."

Melissa asked for a tetanus shot and a small dose of morphine and collected a treatment pack.

"You're not going to treat that animal, are you? You know he must complete his paperwork before you can do anything?"

Melissa flicked a look at the woman who provoked Zach's tantrum.

"When you asked the patient to fill in the paperwork, what did he say?"

"He refused and started throwing things."

"Try to remember what happened before he started throwing things."

"He refused to fill in the paperwork."

"He didn't refuse. Didn't he say that he couldn't fill out the documents?"

The nurse looked confused.

"Let me ask you, which arm and hand are damaged?"

"I don't know. What does it matter?"

Melissa shook her head.

"Nurse, which hand do you write with?"

"This is ridiculous. My right hand, if you have to know."

Melissa reached for a pen and paper over the desk and grabbed the woman's right arm. She shoved the paper and the pen in front of the woman and said, "Sign your name."

The woman struggled to free her hand, but Melissa held on tight.

"Come on, nurse, sign your name. "

"I can't sign my name; you are hanging onto my hand."

Melissa let go of the woman's hand.

"I rest my case. The patient didn't refuse to fill in the documents; he said he couldn't. I'll treat the patient, but having a senior staff member with you might be wise when dealing with a patient next time. You might want to improve your listening skills and empathise with the patients."

Chapter 8

Melissa entered the treatment room armed with the medications and sutures she needed to treat Zach.

"Before we do anything, I need to complete the paperwork."

Once Zach had answered the questions on the document, Melissa was ready to start his treatment.

"Either you grit your teeth or let me cut off this shirt. What's it to be?"

"It's one of the only two shirts I own. Let's see if you can get it off me without me passing out."

Melissa eased his shirt off the uninjured side and then collected the dish that held two shots. Zack's physique surprised Melissa, and, given how he lived, she was stunned by his chiselled chest and tight abdomen. Did the man spend all his money at the gym? Considering the welcome he got from the residents of Fleetwood, she imagined that none of the gym owners would allow him access to their businesses. Even though she averted her eyes quickly, Zach caught her ogling his chest. When he raised his eyebrows, Melissa blushed. Damn, she was supposed to be a healthcare professional, and she gaped at the first attractive man she met in her hometown. She cleared her throat and said,

"I'll do the tetanus shot and the painkiller before we have a go at moving the shirt from your injured arm."

Zach patiently sat as Melissa administered the shots and then gritted his teeth as she attempted to slide the shirt down his injured arm.

"Do you realise this shirt will have a large gash in the sleeve whether I ease it off or not?"

Zach groaned. "Damn, cut it off then; no point in adding to my suffering if I've ruined the shirt anyway."

Melissa snipped away the material and then inspected Zach's arm.

"Sorry, this won't be pretty, but I'll be as careful as possible. Before stitching the wound, let me organise the local anaesthetic to deaden the arm. Sit tight; I'll be back in a tic."

When Melissa approached the nurse's station, the head nurse looked up from her computer.

"How's it going? Is he giving you any trouble?"

"Zach is fine, and if your dippy nurse had used her common sense, he wouldn't have given her any trouble. He needs a lot of stitches, so I'll need about six local anesthetics. Ask whoever mixes them to mix 75% anaesthetic and 25% carb soda. Can someone bring it in when it's ready? I'll clean up the wound and then be ready."

When the previously sobbing nurse brought in the tray with the local anaesthetic, Melissa showed her where to leave the shots and the woman hustled from the room. With the wound thoroughly cleaned, Melissa reached for the first shot.

"This will be a little uncomfortable, but it's better than me stitching without painkillers."

Zach shot up in the chair when Melissa injected the first anaesthetic vial into his arm.

"Shit, if I have to have many of those, I might suggest you stitch without the painkillers."

"Damnation, if that stupid girl mixed it right, it should be uncomfortable, not torturous. I'll be back in a minute."

Melissa stalked from the room. The nurse's desk was vacant, and Melissa slammed her hand on the call button and left it there. When the head nurse hurried to the desk, Mellissa almost snarled at the woman.

"What kind of damn hospital do you lot run? Once I finish with this patient, I intend to report your incompetent nurse. I specifically asked that useless girl to mix the bi card with the anaesthetic, but she didn't. Can I have someone with an ounce of compassion and intelligence to combine the local the way I asked?"

"Dear God, what must you think of us? I'll fix the anaesthetic and then sanction my staff member. It seems Nurse Agers caused the uproar, although I have to say the patient's behaviour was over the top. Is he giving you any trouble?"

"No, I've met Zach before, and I have to say if the nurse had half a brain, he wouldn't have caused the staff any trouble."

The nursing sister handed the doctored anaesthetic shots to Melissa, and she re-entered the treatment room.

Once she sutured the wound, Melissa checked Zach's hand. He had crushed his knuckles and broken at least one of his fingers.

"How did you mess up your hand and damage your arm?"

"I was using the jack, and it slipped, and I couldn't get my arm out from under the truck in time."

"Okay, I've finished here, but we need to x-ray your hand and possibly set it in plaster. I'll get a wheelchair and take you down to radiology."

"I don't need a wheelchair; I can walk."

As Zack rose from the chair, Melissa placed her hand on his chest and pushed him back into the seat.

"It's hospital protocol, so stop pretending you're Superman and let me get the chair."

Melissa pushed the wheelchair along the corridor to the X-ray rooms. When the technician came out, he glared at Zach.

"Are you the bloke that scared Nurse Agers? I should refuse to x-ray your hand and send you home with broken fingers. You can think of the nursing staff who tried to help you whenever you attempted to move them."

Melissa laid her hand on Zach's arm and scowled at the technician.

"Why don't you start this introduction again, Peters? This patient is Zach Hunter, a victim of Nurse Agers's bias and stupidity. I will report her before I leave, and I'm happy to include your name in the complaint procedure if you continue harassing the patient. Your job is to x-ray the patient's hand, not belittle people when you don't know all the facts. Set up the x-ray so Mr Hunter can leave the toxic environment."

The man, Peters, grumbled as he set out the necessary plates, then wheeled Zach into the cubicle. The two men exited the booth a few minutes later, and Peters showed Melissa the image.

"Your patient has two broken fingers and broken his knuckles. It would be best if you bandaged the hand to anchor the broken fingers, but we can't do much with the knuckles except use the hand as little as possible."

Melissa wheeled Zach back to the treatment room and grabbed the bandages to dress Zach's hand. Once she finished dressing his hands, she wheeled Zach towards the nurse's station and presented the on-duty nurse with her prescriptions. The nurse wrapped the medication and placed it in the small cooler before she spoke.

"Because of what occurred here today, I feel it might be better, Miss Anderson, if you change Mr Hunter's bandages daily rather than him presenting here. The nurses are still wary of his temper, and I don't want my staff to suffer distress because a patient can't control himself."

Melissa laughed. "Your staff need to learn how to interact with an injured patient. If I threw a hissy fit every time someone swore at me in the hospital in Maccy, I'd still be curled up in a ball in the corner. I agree that I should change his dressings because I don't believe Mr Hunter should endure the insults and the poor delivery of medical assistance he has already suffered. Rest assured, I will be making an official complaint. Get someone to follow me out so they can retrieve the wheelchair once Mr Hunter is in his vehicle."

Melissa pushed Zach towards the hospital entrance. Today, her priority was to get Zach settled at his home, so she would make an extra trip tomorrow to make her formal complaint. If she shared her grievance with the superintendent, her work environment might be hostile, but Melissa wouldn't back down when she saw a lack of empathy toward injured patients. When Zach saw Melissa's car, he snorted with derision.

"Do you honestly think I can fit in your car? You'd better use my truck and get someone to meet you at the garage to drive you here to collect your vehicle."

Melissa had to admit that she hadn't considered Zach's size; at close to six feet, he would have to curl up to fit in her car. She could drive a stick shift but had never driven a vehicle as big as Zach's truck. After Zach unlocked his truck and climbed in, Melissa adjusted the seat and the mirrors for a few minutes. The drive to the dilapidated building that was Zach's home was a quiet trip.

As she drove, Melissa glanced at Zach and, noticing the pallor of his face and the sweat beading along his hairline, she knew the anaesthetic she had given him at the start of the treatment had stopped working. When she pulled into the driveway of the dilapidated building, Melissa said, "I have some painkillers and antibiotics for you, and even if you are one tough guy, you need to give yourself time to rest. Take the medication every four hours for the first few doses. Afterwards, you can adjust the painkiller dosing interval, but ensure you complete the full course of antibiotics. I will ring my dad to get him to pick me up, and you should rest."

Zach gulped the tablets down with a swallow of water from a bottle on the counter. The more Melissa saw the way Zach lived, the more she worried. People took so many things for granted as everyday essentials, and Zach had none of them. There were no cooking facilities, a refrigerator, or a microwave. How did he eat if the shopkeepers resisted his entering their shops? Pushing aside her worries for the time being, Melissa walked to the property entrance to wait for her father.

Chapter 9

THE TRIP TO THE HOSPITAL had taken longer than she expected, and before Melissa headed into her mother's sick room, her father stopped her with a touch.

"Lissa, we must talk when you get your mum organised."

"I know, but we'll have plenty of time after I get mum set up."

Melissa entered her mother's room with equipment and medications. She set up the stand for the IV bag and pulled out the connections in their sterile bags. She scrubbed her hands, thought of what she had to do, and controlled the urge to make the changes because she needed to consult her mother. Melissa took a seat on the bed next to her mother.

"Mum, I want to put an IV needle in your hand, and the saline drip will hydrate you. Even though you don't complain, I know that you have pain, and until Doctor Winn's medication arrives, I have some morphine to add to the drip. It won't knock you out, but it will take the edge off the pain. Are you happy with that arrangement?"

"Thank you, Lissa; less pain would be welcome."

"Because you will be hydrated, you will have to go to the toilet often, so I'd like to attach a catheter with your permission."

"Please don't do that. I have no control over what happens to my body; putting in the catheter takes even more control."

Melissa looked at her dad, who was watching the proceedings, worriedly.

"Dad, can I have a moment alone with mum?"

"Sure, honey, but don't pressure your mum. We'll manage without it if she doesn't want the catheter."

Melissa turned her attention to her mother when her dad left the room.

"Mum, how do you get to the toilet now?"

"Your dad carries me."

"Dad will have to spend all day and night with you because I can't carry you if you need to go when it's my turn. Dad has done a fantastic job looking after you, but is weary. I'm concerned about his health, and doubling your trips to the toilet may be too much for him. The catheter should be a temporary solution if Doctor Winn's medication works. Please consider it for Dad's sake."

"I lie here without connection to the outside world, and I fear I have become selfish. I've never thought about how this illness is affecting your father. You may use the catheter to relieve him of one task."

"Okay, let's do this before he returns, and I'll also add a small amount of the painkiller when I hook up the IV."

Once Melissa ensured her mother was comfortable, she headed for the kitchen and the discussion she knew would concern Zach Hunter. She tried to organise her thoughts, hoping her father wouldn't issue any ultimatums.

"Okay, Dad, what is on your mind?"

"Tell me why I had to pick you up at the run-down place where your friend Zach lives. I have to say, it concerns me that you're befriending him and spending time alone with him. You can't call for help if you feel threatened because no other people are around."

"I know what the townspeople think about him, but I'm confident there is more to the story. He could have left me at Trader Joe's; it wasn't his job to babysit me, but he did. He fixed my tyre when the sleaze from the tyre service refused, and my trip to the hospital was for Mum's medication. Zach was there because he had injured himself, and the prejudice that followed him in this town affected his treatment at the hospital. Not once have I seen him retaliate or defend himself. He lives in appalling conditions, and even buying food is difficult because the checkout chicks at the supermarket behave as if they expect him to pull out a knife and run around stabbing people."

"Lissa, his welfare is not your concern."

"That raises a question. If Zach were a frail old lady, would you say her welfare is not my concern? Isn't caring about our neighbours and the townsfolk what small communities are about? I studied for four years to become a healthcare professional, and seeing someone suffer goes against the grain. The gossipers in this damn place make the man's life harder than it needs to be. The morning I took him for breakfast, he ate as if it were the first decent meal he'd had in ages. What does he eat if no one serves him? Should I watch him starve to death because it's not my concern? I get the feeling he doesn't trust many people because of the way everyone he encounters treats him. I'm sorry if it upsets you, but if I can help him, I will."

John Anderson saw the conviction on his daughter's face. She was always a stubborn child, and it seemed that trait followed her into adulthood. He could understand what Melissa was saying because, after a close-up look at his living quarters today, he knew the man was doing it tough. Melissa finished the argument before he offered another opinion, and then followed with her comments.

"Zach is my concern for a little while because the nurses at the hospital won't change his bandages, so I offered to do it. I have to change the dressings daily, so I'll be at his place every morning. I wish you could get to know him because he is a good person."

"I trust your judgement, but there's so much talk in the town that it's hard to ignore what people say. His living conditions are squalid; doesn't he get an allowance from the government? Why doesn't he move on if living in Fleetwood is tough?"

"Dad, I understand your concern, but I have one question: who spread the rumour that he is a murderer? Who knew he was settling here in Fleetwood? The rumour and bad reputation must benefit someone, but I can't think who."

Chapter 10

When the package from Simon Winn arrived, Melissa found it hard to control her excitement. Her mother looked so frail that Melissa worried the treatment might be too late to help, but she refused to admit defeat for now. Even though her father had explained to Pam what the drug was supposed to do, Melissa needed to confirm her mother's willingness to undergo the treatment. Pam Anderson was compliant, but Melissa could see resignation rather than optimism.

Melissa checked her mother's temperature, blood pressure and pulse with her stethoscope before hooking up the new saline bag. Watching her father, Melissa hoped that she hadn't provided false hope, but concluded that even if the drug didn't work, her father felt more optimistic than he had for months. Melissa left her mum propped up in bed, listening to an audiobook and headed to Zach's garage. When she arrived, she went to the back of the property and found Zach fiddling with a mechanism. Once he washed up, Melissa removed the bandages and checked the wound, which was clean and free of infection.

"Why aren't you frightened of me? Half the people in the town run when they see me coming. The girls in the supermarket wail like I might go on a murdering rampage, but you treat me like a person."

Zach's question came out of the blue, and Melissa took a minute to answer him.

"That first day we had breakfast, I said I believed there were extenuating circumstances surrounding your conviction, and I still do. Why? Are you going to find a knife and slit my throat? Before taking such drastic action, you might consider that if you murder me, you'll have to submit yourself to Nurse Agers's tender ministrations."

Zach shook his head and smiled.

"You are something else, Mel. While most people think I'm evil, you still believe in me. Thank you for believing. I'm not quite ready to discuss my conviction, but I will eventually share it with you."

Zach watched Melissa leave and shook his head. Her steadfast refusal to believe the gossip that permeated the town buoyed him. Their first meeting, which he admitted was an annoyance, had become a friendship that might grow. For the first time since his imprisonment, Zach felt hopeful.

When Melissa returned home, she checked on her mum and found her sleeping. Without disturbing her, Melissa took her temperature and checked her pulse. Everything was normal, so Melissa went to find her father. Searching the house didn't reveal his presence, and Melissa headed into the garden. She knew her father would not abandon her mother, but he might take some time out for himself if she slept. John Anderson reclined in a deck chair, his face relaxed and calm. His eyes opened to take in Melissa's presence, but he remained seated.

"I needed some time out. Is your mum still asleep?"

"Yes. Mum fought the morphine because she hated losing control, but Doctor Winn's medication must have slipped under her radar."

"I'm not sure if it's mind over matter, but your mum said she felt more comfortable. Lissa, thank you for giving us hope, even if the treatment doesn't work. How did you get her permission to insert the catheter?"

"I explained to her that with the saline drip inserted, she would need to go to the toilet numerous times a day, and if I were the one keeping her company or one of the blue nurses was, we wouldn't be able to move her into the wheelchair. I wish we could afford a lift chair, but they are expensive, and hopefully, it will be redundant soon."

"How did you do with your patient?"

"No problems. Zach asked me why I wasn't afraid of him, and seemed pleased when I expressed my view that there may have been extenuating circumstances surrounding his sentence, and he said there were. He promised to tell me about his conviction soon, so if he allows, I will share it with you so that you can stop worrying."

"I have to admit some concern about you treating him, but if he wanted to attack you, he could have on that first night, and he's had plenty of opportunities since."

"You know how sometimes you meet someone, and they seem familiar? Well, that's how I feel about Zach. I never feel anxious or uncomfortable with him, and I think the community has done him a great disservice by refusing to serve him and banning him from shops. I don't know who leaked the details of his conviction to the people of Fleetwood, but whoever it was, I hope they're happy with the distress they're causing a man who has served time for his crime. Whatever happened to the saying live and let live? Stay out here for a while, and I'll check on mum."

Melissa checked on her mother, and her phone rang as she left the sick room; she diverted her direction and grabbed it before it stopped ringing.

"Miss Andrews?" the voice inquired.

"Yes, Melissa Andrews speaking."

"Ah, good, good. Miss Andrews, it's Tony Hird here, the director of nursing at the Fleetwood General Hospital. I need to meet with you regarding your employment here, and I hope we can make an appointment to meet tomorrow."

"Is there a problem?"

"I'd prefer to discuss your employment in person if you don't mind."

"Okay, I can meet with you in the afternoon, say two o'clock?"

"Good, that fits my schedule. I will see you tomorrow at two."

When Melissa entered the kitchen, her dad noticed her preoccupied expression.

"Is everything all right?"

"I'm not sure. I wonder what the problem is. The call was from Tony Hird, the hospital's director of nursing. He says he needs to talk to me about my employment, so I guess I'll find out tomorrow. At least if I'm meeting him, I can complain about the stupid nurse who wound Zach up and then refused to treat him. They were all for calling security to throw him out when I intervened. Working in a large hospital like Maccy meant I treated many people; some were less compliant than I had hoped, but we managed to work through the challenges. The nursing staff here have it so easy; they've never learned to handle frustrating patients. I know that complaining may make the working environment tricky, but I can't ignore how the nurse treated Zach. What if I hadn't been there?"

"I can understand your concern about the nurse. Let's hope there isn't a problem with your employment."

Chapter 11

Melissa started the following day with a morning check of her mother's vital signs, then dished up a weak broth a neighbour had delivered to entice her mother to eat. Halfway through the bowl, Pam claimed she was full, but even a tiny amount of food was better than what she had eaten before the change in medication. After giving her mother a bed bath and setting up the newest audiobook, Melissa realised she wouldn't complete her tasks for the day unless she hurried. Despite Tony Hird's call, Melissa couldn't imagine any problems delaying her start date, so this afternoon she needed to find her scrubs and iron them.

When Melissa pulled into the driveway of Zach's dilapidated building, she shook her head. What on earth convinced him to buy this place? Oh well, one subject at a time and today, she intended to get Zach to tell her about his conviction. Melissa called out as she entered the building, and Zach's reply had her heading towards the back room.

"Hi, your friendly personal nurse calling."

Zach smiled, and Melissa felt her heart skip a beat. How had she become attached to the one man in Fleetwood that nobody else trusted? Once she placed the bandages, salve, and antibacterial swabs on the couch, she sat beside him and unwrapped the dressings covering Zach's wound. They chatted as she worked; Zach asked after her mother and said he had a surprise for her when she finished. Melissa was uncertain what the surprise might be, but before she let him drag her away to look at the surprise, she wanted him to explain what led to his incarceration.

"Zach, before you show me your surprise, will you tell me how you ended up in jail?"

When Zach didn't answer, Melissa sighed. She hoped he trusted her enough to tell her the details of his incarnation, but it seemed he didn't.

"I'm sorry if you don't want to explain what happened. I understand that it must be difficult to talk about it. Forget I asked."

Zack ran his hand through his shoulder-length hair.

"I'm afraid you will think less of me once I tell you what happened. I will miss your friendship and optimism."

"Zach, the only way I will think less of you is if you tell me you planned to murder your victim and lie in wait to commit your crime."

"No, I didn't, but there is a back story to go with what happened, so bear with me. I had a happy childhood; I had an older brother, Michael, a loving mum and a great dad. Michael and I would sit on the back step at night, waiting for Dad to come home from work. When he arrived, he kissed Mum hello and then played with Michael and me until dinner. Some nights, he read a bedtime story, and Michael and I were sure we were the luckiest kids in the neighbourhood. The year I turned eleven, everything changed. Brandis Industries, where Dad worked, was taken over by another company, which downsized, sacking 50 men. My dad was an engineer, and finding another job in our area was nearly impossible. Many families who rented their homes packed up and left, but my parents had a mortgage on our house, and they didn't think they would be able to sell the house with so many workers departing from town."

Zach stopped his narration and sat with his eyes closed. He pushed the hair off his face and continued.

"Dad got a job as a maintenance man at another company, and he hated the job. He had to repair malfunctioning or broken machines, including toilets and bathrooms. Dad began calling into the local pub for a drink before coming home, so he arrived later and no longer played with us or read us bedtime stories. We were shocked the first night he arrived, rolling drunk and aggressive. Mum rushed Michael and me off to bed as Dad shouted and screamed insults at her. His behaviour escalated until the first night he hit Mum. It seemed that once the man had crossed that line, there was no stopping him. Every night after that, he'd roll home, slap, and punch my mother. Mum spared Michael and me the trauma of watching because she fed us and sent us to bed before Dad got home. One night, I decided to help mum, and when I entered the kitchen, her face was bleeding, and my father continued hitting her. I jumped on his back and beat him with my fists, but he threw me off and assaulted me. The medical staff at the hospital tried to convince our mother to leave Dad, but she refused, saying that he didn't mean to harm us; it was just frustration with his job. No amount of pleading on our part made Mum change her mind, so when Michael turned eighteen and got a job, he moved out and told me to keep my head down for a few years, and then I could move in with him. After moving out of the house, I checked on Mum every Saturday because that was when Dad went to the footy. The Saturday it happened, he changed his mind and didn't go to the football.

When I arrived, I could hear the distinct sound of slaps and punches. I raced into the kitchen, and Mum was a bloody mess, curled on the floor, trying to protect herself. I needed a weapon because I knew I couldn't tackle him without one, so I grabbed the first thing that came to hand: a frying pan. I swung it at Dad's head, hoping to knock him out so I could call the ambulance. The police arrived with the ambulance, and I sat on the floor near Mum while the paramedics tried to save her life. I wanted to go to the hospital with Mum, but the police wouldn't let me because the ambos declared that Dad was dead after a quick check. Without aiming, I had flung the frypan at him, hit him in the temple, and the bastard was dead. So while Mum headed to the hospital, the police arrested me for murder and shoved me into the back of a patrol car."

Zach turned to look at Melissa, sure that he would see disgust and condemnation on her face. What he saw staggered him; tears rolled down Melissa's face, her heart breaking for the young man who tried to save his mother.

"Surely they couldn't charge you with murder if you were protecting your mother?"

"My solicitor wanted them to charge my father's death as death by misadventure, but the district attorney tried to big-note himself. My solicitor badgered him to reduce the murder charge to involuntary manslaughter, and I pleaded guilty, hoping to get a reduced sentence. I did four of my six-year sentence."

"What happened to Michael and your mother?"

"My mother was in a coma for three months, but eventually recovered. I haven't seen either her or Michael since my sentence. My criminal record doesn't reflect well on Michael's business, and he suggested a new beginning in a town where the population don't know about my conviction. The suggestion might have merit, but my reputation seemed to precede me. I assume my mother doesn't want to see me because I killed her husband."

"If a woman stays with a man who beats her, that is sad. But a woman who stays with a man who will assault his kids is selfish and negligent. Your mother should be here thanking you for saving her life, and Michael, the snob, should be here thanking you for saving his mother's life. Thank you for telling me; I can't express how sad I feel about what happened to you."

Zach seemed to rally. "Can I show you my surprise now?"

Melissa followed Zach through a door to a workshop, and before her was an old wheelchair. Damn, how did she decline what was a kind offer from a man everyone concluded had no kindness in him?

Zach snorted a laugh. "Don't ever play poker, sweetheart. Your face shows every thought that passes through your pretty little head. Please sit in the chair."

Melissa sat in the chair, and when Zach walked behind her, she wondered what he was doing. When the seat started to rise, Melissa sat, stunned. The chair's height, according to Zach, could be varied. Returning to the front of the chair, he fiddled with the armrest and raised it so it wouldn't impede the person sitting in it.

"You said you couldn't afford a chair lift, but I thought this might help. Moving the arm and raising the chair level with your mother's bed would allow her to slide across, or even if she needs help, it would be easier than lifting her."

Melissa rose from the chair, and Zach showed her how to raise and lower it. With a whoop of joy, Melissa threw her arms around Zach and hugged him.

"This is great, thank you. We will need your truck to take it to my parents' place, but they will be thrilled. They can meet you tomorrow and thank you personally."

"I can't go to your parents' house. They'll take one look at me and throw me out."

"My parents don't judge people on their appearance, but have a haircut and a shave if it worries you."

Zach grimaced. "The barber will be like everyone else in town; he will refuse to serve me."

"The barber is my Uncle Charlie. Let me talk to him and see what he says. I have to go to the hospital, but you can walk to the barber's shop in about an hour after I've talked to him."

Chapter 12

Her trip to the barbershop proved fruitful for Melissa. After some persuasion, her uncle agreed to her request, and she paid her uncle for the upcoming visit.

"What, the bloke lets you pay his way?"

"No, he doesn't know that I am paying, but fifty dollars for a haircut and a shave is cheaper than two or three thousand for a lift chair for mum."

Happy that she had Zach's barber visit sorted, Melissa headed for the hospital.

Melissa left the hospital, stunned at what had happened. Mr Hird explained that Mrs Cartwright had offered to fund the intensive care neonatal unit if the hospital admin didn't hire Melissa. Even though she had a contract, the man explained that they would defend their right to change their mind about her employment, and if she took them to court, the proceedings would be expensive and could drag on for a long time. It seemed James had his mother's backing in trying to persuade Melissa to adopt his perspective. If James imagined he could bully her into agreeing to whatever mad scheme he had devised, he was in for a shock. Didn't James know her well enough to realise he couldn't bully her into changing her mind?

Since her arrival home, nothing had gone right. First, James ' engagement party, then her mother's terminal illness, and now she was unemployed. Melissa wanted to scream at the world's unfairness, but instead of burdening her father, she headed for the park. No one would see her if she sat on a park bench and bawled her eyes out. Melissa chose a bench on the outskirts of the park. Nearby, there were no picnic tables, barbeques or amusements for children, so there should be no interruptions from nosy strangers. Melissa took a deep breath and closed her eyes.

"Mel?"

The sound of Zach's voice brought her out of her daze. She looked up and saw the concern in his eyes. She would fall apart if she thought about her life, so she asked about the haircut and shave he hadn't had.

"Don't tell me Uncle Charlie refused to cut your hair?"

"He told me to return just before closing time; that's where I'm going now. But don't try to distract me. Why are you sitting on a park bench alone?"

Melissa sighed.

"I wanted some privacy to curse and rant and cry. Since I returned, everything has gone wrong. James dumped me publicly in the most humiliating experience ever; my friends kept his cheating a secret, my mum has cancer, and now I no longer have a job. Mrs Cartwright offered to fund the hospital's neonatal unit if they fired me. How much worse could it get? I can't sob on Dad's shoulders because I have to support him, and Brett is the least sympathetic person I know, so I decided here was as good as any place to have a meltdown."

"I have wide shoulders if you want to cry."

Zach opened his arms, and Melissa stepped into his embrace. Zach rested his bandaged arm around her waist and patted her on the back. The tears flowed, eventually becoming gut-wrenching sobs. The sobs finally ceased, and with some hiccoughing breaths, Melissa gained control. Zach didn't release her immediately, and she remained wrapped in his arms. When she stepped back, she gave a shaky smile.

"Thank you for that. You have great shoulders to cry on. For some reason, I feel safe with you. Even that first night that you sat next to me, I could feel your body heat, and I felt safe. I'd better go home and tell my parents I'm unemployed, and you had better hurry to the barbers before Uncle Charlie thinks you're not coming and closes up."

Zach leaned forward, placed a light kiss on her cheek, and then turned and hurried away. Melissa touched her cheek where Zach had kissed her, aware she was beginning to care for him.

When Melissa returned home, she prepared dinner while reviewing her day. Her father was keeping her mother company, but when she was ready to serve the meal, she would need to share the reason for her dismissal from the hospital. Once Melissa shared her news with her family, she wanted to explain Zach's incarceration and let her parents know he would visit tomorrow. She expected her parents would listen to her explanation, but convincing Brett was another matter.

After helping her mother drink most of the smoothie she had made, Melissa served her father and brother. Her mother's increased appetite gave the family a sense of optimism, and Melissa decided to enjoy the meal before she broached the tricky subject. Unfortunately, Brett didn't have any qualms about causing a fuss over tea, and as soon as they were seated at the table, he launched into a tirade.

"I had your ex accost me in the street as I left work because a runner saw you and the convict making out in the park and couldn't wait to spread the news. What the hell is wrong with you, Melissa? Are you going out of your way to get the whole town offside, not to mention the trouble the Cartwrights could cause you? Stay away from the guy."

Melissa sighed. "I wanted to eat dinner before sharing disturbing news with you guys. Trust you to go at the topic like a bull at a gate. Leave the subject alone, and I will answer your allegations when we finish eating. I don't want to explain myself ten times, so when we finish here, I suggest we join mum, and I'll clear up the issues then."

Brett grumbled at Melissa's response, and her father looked concerned, but she had no intention of explaining to her dad and Brett and then repeating herself to her mother.

Melissa propped her mother up in bed, and the Anderson men took the chairs they had carried in from the kitchen. Pam Anderson looked confused at the sudden influx of her family, but before commencing her explanation, Melissa checked her mother's vital signs. Satisfied that everything was as it should be, Melissa explained the reason for the meeting to her mother.

"Mum, I have some things I want to tell you, and even though Brett made accusations at dinner, it was easier for me to deal with everything at once. If this tires you out too much, please let me know, and I will finish with my news later."

Pam Anderson smiled. "I haven't been so interested in what you have to say in such a long time, but now I have the energy to listen, so please proceed."

"Okay. I'll deal with Brett's accusation first. At dinner, Brett said that James accosted him as he left work and told him to warn me away from Zach. A nosy runner had seen Zach and me in the park and reported to James that we were making out in public. Dad always says," Never let the truth get in the way of a good story." I met Zach in the park by accident. I had just had some bad news, and on top of all that had happened since I arrived home, I needed some time out and the ability to cry without distressing you and Dad. Zach offered me his shoulder to cry on, and the only kiss was a cheek kiss as he left. Does that answer your allegation, Brett?"

"Yeah, that explains what happened, but not why you keep spending time with this bloke. He is a murderer, and you place yourself in danger whenever you see him."

"He isn't a murderer, and I'll prove that in a minute, but aren't you interested in my bad news?"

John Anderson spoke before they became more distracted by Brett's statement.

"Lissa, even if Brett is side-tracked by James, please tell us what news distressed you?"

"Do you remember when James visited the house and issued threats about his mother's power over the town?"

John nodded.

"Well, today I met with Simon Hird at the hospital. He said Mrs Cartwright had pledged to match the hospital's funds dollar for dollar, enabling them to build the neonatal intensive care unit. Her one condition was that the hospital tear up my contract, and they did. I am now unemployed."

Pam Anderson let out a gasp. "They can't do that, can they?"

"Legally, no, they can't, but Mr Hird said that if I challenged the dismissal, he could tie us up in court for an extended period, and even if we won, the hospital would be a toxic workplace because my employment would mean Mrs Cartwight would withdraw her funds. It appears that James has his mother's support in making me cease my contact with Zach."

Brett shook his head. "Well, for god's sake, woman, stop seeing the man."

"I can't stop seeing Zach because the nurses at the hospital won't change his dressings, and somebody has to do it. Besides, Brett, do you want me to align myself with Mrs Cartwright's wishes? She will put more pressure on me until I'm willing to be James's mistress and accommodate him while he is married to that other woman. Is that what you want?"

The occupants of the room remained silent after Melissa's statement. When John Anderson finally spoke, he said, "How did the woman get enough power to manipulate people like she does? I'm not sure what she has in mind in the form of coercion, but no daughter of mine will become a whore just because her spoiled son wants to have his cake and eat it."

"And if I bow to James's demand or Mrs Cartwright's ploys, I would have no option but to become a kept woman. After all the time I've known James, I can't believe he would try to force me to do something he must know I'd hate. But now that we've got that out of the way, I have the truth about Zach's incarceration. He shared it with me earlier, and I want to share it today. It's a complicated story; are you up to this, mum?"

"Yes, Lissa, I'm fine."

As Melissa related Zach's story, she felt a shift in her family's emotions. Her father, who rarely swore and was a quiet and controlled man, let out a string of words she was sure had never left his mouth before; the tears rolled down her mother's face, and Brett stared with appalled fascination.

"So, tell me, is Zach a murderer?"

"Why doesn't the town know the real story?"

"Dad, the story is in the public record, but I believe the lies profit someone, although I have no idea who or how. On a lighter note, Zach has made a present for you, Mum, which will benefit Dad. Can he bring it over tomorrow morning?"

Pam Anderson smiled. "We would be pleased to meet your new friend. Invite him for morning tea or lunch so we can thank him for his present. I'm excited to see what this young man has made us, but just now, I might have a rest and listen to my story."

Melissa made her mother comfortable, and she and Brett left the room. When she entered the kitchen, she collected the kettle and set it to boil while preparing the teapot. Brett remained quiet as he watched his sister prepare the tea, but his voice held an apology when he spoke.

"The town and I have all believed the circulated lies. Dad said you had developed good people skills while in the city, and it appears you were the only person who saw the man for who he really was. It shames me to admit that I listened to the rumours and convicted him of a crime he didn't commit."

"Thanks, Brett; I appreciate you saying that."

"So, what's the present?"

Melissa grinned at her brother. "You'll have to wait and see."

Chapter 13

Melissa pulled the last batch of scones from the oven and placed them on the cooling rack. She surveyed the results of her early morning start; cakes and slices adorned the benchtop. After their morning tea, she would give Zach an assortment of cakes to take home, freeze some for later and leave the rest for her father and brother to enjoy each afternoon. John Anderson kept his wife company, and Melissa entered the bedroom to say goodbye. By the time she changed Zach's bandages and they loaded up the wheelchair, it would be morning tea time.

Anticipation raced through Melissa's body as she approached Zach's rundown building. What would he look like with short hair and a shave? Even with his unkempt appearance, he was a good-looking man, but she anticipated he would be devastatingly handsome with a cleanup. As she pulled into his driveway, she saw the wheelchair behind his truck; the awkward shape and the chair's size meant he needed help loading it.

When Zach strolled out from the back of the garage, Melissa gaped at him. His hair was short on the sides and back with more length at the front, and her Uncle Charlie had trimmed his scraggly beard to give him heavy stubble. He smirked at her as he approached, and she couldn't drag her gaze from his face.

"Oh, my. I knew there was a good-looking bloke under all that hair, but you would look good on the cover of a magazine. Who knew my grumpy companion was drop-dead gorgeous?"

Zach blushed, and that delighted Melissa. She scanned the rest of his body and realised that he had worn the jeans and shirt she had searched for at the op shop.

"Okay, handsome, let's dress your arm."

"Sure, but we need to discuss you paying for my haircut and shaving. I have some money, but Charlie said you paid for the cut and shave. Are you trying to un-man me? What do you think your uncle thought of you shelling out the money?"

"Ah, I'm sorry if I injured your pride, and Uncle Charlie said the same thing about the money. I'm happy for you to repay the fifty dollars, but only if you let me pay you a couple of thousand for the chair. The lift chair is worth more than the barber's cost, and I told Uncle Charlie that yesterday. He recognised the sense in what I said, so I hope you can, too."

Zach grumbled about bossy females and sat on the couch while Melissa redressed his wound. After so many days, they had the bandaging down pat, and soon Melissa packed her equipment and walked out to Zach's truck. They managed to manoeuvre the chair onto the truck's tray between them, and Zach secured it with ropes.

"Will I un-man you if I offer to drive?"

"God, woman, you're a pain. You know I can't drive the truck yet, so get in the driver's seat, and let's do this."

The drive to Melissa's place was silent; she wished she could ease his nerves. As she drove, he bounced his leg up and down, and when they pulled into her driveway, she said,

"I promise, Zach, my parents will not be rude or give you a hard time."

Zach grunted as he jumped from the truck and stood at the front of the vehicle, waiting for Melissa. When the front door opened, John Anderson watched his daughter and the man she had befriended and was pleasantly surprised at the man's appearance. The rumours around town described him as resembling a homeless person, but the man who stood with Melissa was neat and tidy.

"Dad, can you give Zach a hand with the chair?"

John Anderson walked down the step toward the stranger. He helped remove the wheelchair from the truck's tray and raised an eyebrow in question at his daughter. Mel laughed at her father's expression and said, "Zach told me never to play cards because my opponents will be able to read me like a book. I must get that trait from you, Dad, but I promise the chair answers our prayers. Let me introduce Zach Hunter, my friend who has fueled the gossip in Fleetwood."

When John held out his hand to shake, Zach held up his hand to show John.

"Ah, sorry. Handshaking is beyond me at the moment.".

"Tell me why this wheelchair differs from your mother's, Lissa."

Melissa sat in the wheelchair and smiled at Zach.

"Do your thing, my friend."

When Zach raised the wheelchair, John Anderson's mouth gaped open. After lowering the seat, Zach showed John how to remove the armrest to make sliding from the bed easier.

"And with your injured hand, you made this for Pam?"

Melissa had never seen her father so choked up, and she was thankful that she had insisted Zach meet her parents.

"Mel has helped me more than once, and seeing as this was something I could do, I wanted to repay her in a small way. It doesn't look flash, but it should do the job."

John shook his head. "Lissa said you were a good person, and she was right. Thank you, Zach, for your kindness. We'd better introduce you to Pam before she tries to get out of bed and introduce herself."

Melissa led the way and held the door wide so Zach could wheel the lift chair into the room. Her mum's face was flushed, and she looked excited about her visitor and the chair. After checking her mother's vital statistics, Melissa entered the kitchen to plate the cakes and biscuits for their morning tea. When her dad followed her into the room, she looked over her shoulder at him.

"Thanks, Lissa. I'm glad you ignored all the rumours about Zach. His visit has revived your mum. I know she will be tired later in the day, but she is happy and interested."

Melissa nodded. "A new face is always welcome when a person is confined to bed. Even though the invalid feels grateful to the helpers, a new face adds excitement to their day."

Left alone, Pam and Zach sat awkwardly, and then Pam laughed.

"Melissa said you were misunderstood, but didn't say you were a knock-out. I can't believe the ladies in town aren't chasing you around and accosting you in quiet places."

Zach coughed and then laughed. "And she didn't say you were a feisty lady, either."

"Zach, I hope you don't mind, but Melissa told us your story. I understand how confused and scared you were when the police arrested you. Losing control of your life is frightening; I know because I lie here with a loving family making daily decisions for me. I try to look brave so they don't worry, but I'm scared about what happens next. It's terrifying not to know what to expect."

Zach leant over and took Pam's hand.

"The only difference between your situation and mine is that you have a family that supports you; my family made themselves scarce when I was arrested and never visited me in prison. But even with support, the unknown can be terrifying, and I guessed you put on a brave face for your family."

Zach gave a slight grin. "Mel knows how good my shoulder is for crying on, and you're welcome to use it when you need a cry but don't want to worry your family."

Melissa interrupted their conversation when she and her dad walked in carrying a veritable feast. She noticed that Zach held her mother's hand but made no comment; whatever had happened between her mother and Zach, they had made a connection. The conversation and the food flowed, and it excited Melissa to see her mother crumble a muffin and eat a small portion. When her mother was tired, Melissa rechecked her vital signs, preparing to settle her for a rest.

"Zach, come and revisit me soon. A change of face will be welcome, even though Lissa and John are wonderful at looking after me. A handsome man is always welcome."

Zach smiled and agreed.

John suggested they retire to the kitchen, primarily so that Melissa could top up the biscuits. The conversation covered general topics with refreshed cups of tea and coffee until Zach said, "What happens now you can't work at the hospital?"

Melissa shrugged. "I haven't given it much thought. I might have to work as a checkout chick at the supermarket."

John said, "Over my dead body. You didn't do all that studying and spend four years in the city to come home and not use your skills. There must be a way around the self-important Cartwrights."

"Mel, is there another doctor in town that you could work with?"

"I'm not sure. Doctor Burns is our local GP, but with him working as my parents' primary medical practitioner, it might not be the best option."

John Anderson said, "It never entered my mind that you could work with an established clinic. What about Doctor Prescott? I heard he is looking to retire. If you set up in his rooms, you'd already have clients to treat. The bank would probably give you a loan for an established business."

"That sounds like a possibility. It'll depend on how much doctor Prescott charges; some clients will want to find another doctor, but most would probably remain with the clinic. Will you come with me, Dad, to talk to Doctor Prescott?"

"Sure, and if it sounds feasible, we can make an appointment with the bank's loan manager."

Melissa was excited when she arrived at Zach's place the next day. She brimmed with enthusiasm as she recounted her conversation with her father and Doctor Prescott after the surgery closed. Her enthusiasm amused Zach, and he was grateful she had an option for her medical skills. Doctor Prescott was ready to retire, and his suggestion that Melissa work with him before taking over the clinic made perfect sense. They agreed on a tentative price, and Melissa and her dad had an appointment with their local bank manager. After so many disappointments, it looked like Melissa's luck had changed.

Before Melissa left Zach's place, her dad rang to ask to speak to Zach. Melissa raised her eyebrows at the unusual request but passed the phone to Zach. While she could only hear at the end of the conversation, it seemed her dad needed help with something, and he hoped Zach could provide it. When Zach hung up, Melissa questioned him.

"What did my dad want?"

"Your mum's medical bed has arrived, and while he can put the bed together, he can't work out how to get the mechanical component attached and working. Can you give me a ride to your place?"

Once they arrived at her house, Melissa checked on her mum and left Zach and her dad to their own devices. The conversations she could hear from the kitchen amused her as the two struggled to fit the lifting device. Zac's hand impeded him, so he gave John instructions while keeping his hands away from the mechanism. Melissa took the opportunity to cook a quiche and a casserole for lunch. She doubted that Zach ate well, and his lack of amenities concerned her. The narrow-mindedness of her hometown angered her, and she knew Zach suffered at the hands of the local shopkeepers, and it would please her to supplement his food intake.

Chapter 14

After the mechanism was attached to the bed and was working well, Melissa, her mother, and the two men enjoyed a leisurely lunch. Pam Anderson was eating small portions of the meals Melissa prepared, and her face was not as grey as it had been. Melissa and her dad had an appointment with the bank, so Zach offered to sit with Pam while they were away. Zach's connection with his mother and the care he showed her warmed Melissa's heart. How had this good man been so maligned by those who knew him?

On their way to the bank, her dad said, "I've just met Zach, but I can see why you trusted him even before you knew his story. He's here by himself, trying to battle with people who have shunned and mistrusted him, and his family is nowhere in sight. While you recounted what happened to him, I felt like locating his brother and mother and slapping them both. I wonder why he stays if he doesn't have the money to fix the building he lives in?"

"I know his brother told him to start over in a new town where no one knew him. I can't believe that his family would abandon him as they did, and I must say that if I ever meet them, I will be hard-pressed to be civil."

While waiting for the bank manager, Melissa reflected on her father's comments about Zach living in Fleetwood. She might ask about his plans the next time she dressed his arm.

The bank manager listened to Melissa's proposal and nodded in agreement as she listed the benefits of taking over an existing business. The manager gave Melissa a verbal agreement but requested a list of assets and last year's financial records. John and Melissa returned home after a quick phone call to Doctor Prescott. While her dad put the kettle on, Melissa told her mum and Zach about their successful application. Pam Anderson looked pleased with the news for the clinic, but Melissa could see that her mom was tired. After checking her vitals, she settled her mum for a nap and met the men in the kitchen. They chatted for a few minutes, and then John said, "Zach, forgive me if I offended you, but why did you buy that rundown building if you couldn't afford the repairs?"

Zach gazed down at his cup and then straightened his shoulders.

"When you hear how I came to be the owner of that rubble, you will think I'm a fool."

Melissa reached out and put her hand on Zach's arm.

"Remember when I asked about your conviction, and before you explained, you said I'd mistrust and loathe you? Well, I didn't, and I assure you neither my dad nor I will think you are a fool, whatever the circumstances."

Zach nodded. "Well, here goes. When I was in jail, I decided to start a mechanical repair shop upon my release. I took a course in small business and refreshed my mechanic's qualification, and then I needed a place to set up. I logged onto real estate websites to search for the right place.

When I found a suitable building, I did some research, and with only one competitor here in town, I was confident I could make a go of the business. I contacted the real estate agent, who sent more photos and put me in touch with a solicitor. The pictures of the building the bloke sent me showed an abandoned building, but the paintwork was spot-on, and the inside was dusty but well-equipped.

The sale included some tools, pulleys, and other mechanical equipment. I asked why the owners abandoned the place, and the real estate guy told me that the man who ran the business had died in a car accident, and the family had walked away from the district. We agreed on a price, and the solicitor told me I was making a great purchase, but

I wanted someone to keep an eye on the property. I rang Michael and explained what I wanted to do, but I needed someone to look at the place to see if my plan had any downsides.

Michael agreed to look at the place, and I waited for his report. He said he was tied up but would make the trip soon. When the okay came, I was excited and believed Michael's assessment. I signed the paperwork, and we finalised the sale. The day I collected the keys was the proudest of my life, but when I saw the place, I knew the others had scammed me. I rang Michael to ask him why, after checking the building, he let me buy what amounted to a derelict building. It turns out that Michael didn't check the building; he rang the solicitor, who told him it was a solid buy. I fronted the agent and the solicitor to try and get my money back, but they just laughed and said they had been trying to get rid of the building for years."

Melissa groaned."Dear God, that's awful. Does your brother feel any remorse? Will he provide the money for repairs?"

Zac shook his head. "No, he won't provide money to fix this place, and his remorse stretched to a weak apology. So, now I live in a dump similar to a third-world country."

After rifling through a drawer, John rose from the table and returned with a pad and pen.

"You are not a fool; you are a trusting person who never considered that a supposedly reputable agent and the solicitor would perpetuate a scam of this nature. Lissa said at one stage that whoever released the supposed details of your incarceration must have had an ulterior motive. The motive is to keep people away from you so no one would know what they did. Well, bad luck for them that Lissa is a good judge of character, and while we were scared you might murder her, she was confident there were extenuating circumstances. Have you got the pictures and the documents for the sale?"

"Yes, why?"

"Because my solicitor and you and I will get your money back. Do you mind if I have an independent valuer to assess the building's worth properly?"

"No, but how will you make them return my funds?"

John grinned. "A little bit of blackmail goes a long way. What they did is a fraud, and the police will be interested, as will the regulatory bodies for real estate and lawyers."

Melissa, who was silent during this exchange, said, "Zach, I doubt that I could be civil if I met your brother. My opinion of him is very low. He has let you down in so many aspects of your life while he sits pretty in his office."

Zach sighed. "I guess I am a fool; I keep expecting my family to do the right thing, and they continue to disappoint. The next time I consider asking them for help, remind me why it is a bad idea."

Chapter 15

The next few days were busy for Melissa, Zach and John. Melissa spent time collating Doctor Prescott's patient numbers and his weekly takings. The doctor's financial paperwork was cumbersome, and Melissa vowed to move everything to an online portal when she took over. She had an appointment to talk to the bank manager later. Her dad and Zach met with Brandon Dixon, her father's friend and attorney. With his help, they concentrated on getting the agent and solicitor to refund Zach's money.

The meeting with the agent and the solicitor recommended to Zach was at the solicitor's premises. When John and Brandon entered the room with Zach, the solicitor bristled.

"What the devil is happening? Mr Hunter asked for legal advice."

Brandon said, "That's right, he wants legal advice, but we are waiting on someone else to help us."

When Jeff Betson, the real estate agent, arrived at the door, he hesitated, and his eyes flew straight to his solicitor friend.

"What is going on?"

Brandon smiled. "Ah, now we are all here so that we can get started. Betson, you and your mate, Thompson, have perpetuated fraud against my client, Zach Hunter. You knowingly misled Zach about the state of the business he was buying, and I feel confident that the real estate institute and the legal advice body would be interested to see how you operate."

Betson and Thompson locked eyes. Betson was the first to speak.

"You can't prove we defrauded your client; it's his word against ours, and a murdering criminal like him will have no hope of convincing others that we did the wrong thing."

Bradon laid his briefcase on the table and drew out a folder with Zach's name.

"I think you have miscalculated. Mr Hunter has a copy of all his communications with you, along with photos of the building and equipment he believed he was purchasing. If you continue to deny the scam you pulled, we will conclude this meeting. Be prepared to answer questions when your industry bodies come calling. I guarantee there is enough evidence to have you both disbarred, and once that occurs, I will ask the police to investigate. A term in jail might make you rethink your business practices."

Thompson blustered. "There's no need to be hasty. I'm certain Jeff and I can offer compensation."

Brandon Dixon smiled. "That's more like it. An independent assessment valued the property at $50,000. You will make restitution to the sum of one hundred and fifty thousand to reimburse Zach the difference in the actual price and the inflated price you charged him."

Betson and Thompson nodded. John and Zach had silently sat as Brandon dealt with the legal aspects of the former sale, but now John spoke.

"There is one other thing you must do to make this right. Unless you write a letter to the editor apologising to Zach for making false claims about the reason for his incarceration, we will sue you for slander. Melissa, my daughter, said that the person spreading lies about Zach had an invested interest in keeping the community from befriending him, and she was right. You didn't want anyone to befriend him, so he couldn't share the reasons for buying that dilapidated building, but you never counted on my compassionate daughter meeting Zach."

Betson and Thompson looked ill, and Brandon put the final nail in the coffin. "Gentlemen, when you finish the draft of your letter to the editor, you must run it past my office before the paper prints it."

"I will check with Zach; if the refund isn't in his account by the week's end, I will follow through with a call to the police and the regulatory bodies you belong to."

It astounded Zach that, with his friend's help, the untenable position he found himself in was resolved. He now needed to decide whether to undertake the massive renovations on the building or take the money and run. He would discuss his options with John, who had turned out to be an excellent mentor. When Zach first saved Melissa, he complained about her constant incursions into his life, but now he realised she was his saving grace. Not only had she befriended him, but she also shared her family with him, and for that, he would always be grateful. Watching the Anderson family interact with one another made him realise that his mother and brother failed him in so many ways. Their desertion of him during the trial and prison sentence compounded their neglect. Zach rarely asked Michael for help, but being told that he had checked the building and it was fine and the suggestion that he start again in another town, saddened and angered him. He never asked his family for assistance; instead, he followed the recommendations John put forward.

At last, things in the Anderson family began to settle. Pam was eating more and had more energy, and with her improvements, Melissa felt more confident that the medication would provide the required reprieve from cancer eating at her mother's body. John Anderson took Zach under his wing, and the pair shortlisted the repairs needed to rejuvenate the garage and provide Zach with an income. Once the agent and solicitor's press release about Zach's prison sentence became public, the community seemed to change its mind.

While her dad and Zach planned for the repairs, Melissa saw less and less of her friend. She would remove the bandages the following morning, and Melissa looked forward to having him to herself for a short while. When she arrived at the garage, she could see the changes that her father and his friends from the men's shed had made. The men had cleared the parking area, and the fence surrounding the building now stood erect. Melissa wandered to the back of the building, and Zach sat on a new sofa, a drink in his hand. The upgrade in the furniture made her smile; at last, Zach had something to call his own.

Seated next to Zach, Melissa unwrapped the wound and checked it for any signs of infection. She snipped and removed the stitches with her surgical scissors and tweezers. When she removed the last stitches, Melissa swabbed the area and rolled a bandage sleeve over the wound. Before Zach could move, Melissa straddled his legs and lowered her mouth to kiss him. The kiss was brief, and much to her embarrassment, there was no response from Zach. Mortified by his lack of interest, Melissa eased herself out of her seat and collected her equipment.

"Sorry, I've wanted to do that since you gave me your shoulder to cry on. Don't worry; it won't happen again."

Taking a deep breath to prevent the tears from falling, Melissa turned away from Zach. She had taken a step away when a large hand gripped her arm, and she swung around, expecting to be the subject of a tirade and a scowling face.

"Sorry, sweetheart, you don't get to kiss me and then run away."

He pulled her close, her breasts pressed against his chest as he grabbed a handful of hair and tilted her face. The kiss was soft and dreamy, but when his hand wrapped around her waist, he pulled her body flush against himself and deepened the kiss. Melissa gripped his biceps to prevent herself from collapsing, the kiss robbing her of all conscious thoughts. When Zach slid his mouth to her neck to nibble the tender skin behind her ear, Melissa groaned. Cupping her cheek, Zach stepped back and watched as Melissa tried to focus her attention on the man who had just rocked her world.

"I've wanted to do that since I carried you here and laid you on that old couch. I never made a move because I didn't think you'd be interested, but why did you wait until now?"

"Five minutes ago, you ceased to be my patient. I'd hate to have you report me to the medical board for unprofessional conduct."

Melissa's phone rang, and she grimaced.

"Can we resume our conversation after I take this?"

Zach gave her a cocky grin. "I'm not sure what you want to resume, but I'm up for anything."

When Melissa answered her phone, her dad's voice was the last person she expected to hear. As a rule, he rarely phoned anyone, so panic set in immediately.

"Oh gosh, Dad, has something happened to Mum? Is she alright?"

"Calm down, Lissa. I'm sorry; I didn't mean to scare you. I wanted to talk to Zach, and as he doesn't have a phone, I thought you might still be with him."

Melissa rolled her eyes and handed the phone to Zach. After a short conversation, Zach clicked off the call and gave her the phone.

"Can I have a rain check? Your dad wants me to pick up some stuff from the hardware, and then he will help me clear out the reception area."

"Gee, now I have to share you with my family, do I?"

Zach looped his arm around her neck and kissed her on the cheek.

"You have no idea how happy it makes me that your family accepts me. After the neglect my family has shown me, I'm pleased to have your family's support."

Melissa leaned up and kissed his mouth.

"I'm pleased they like you too, but I'd better let you go before my dad arrives and we're still making out."

As Zach drove away, Melissa climbed into her car. She crossed her fingers for a moment, praying that all the bad things had finished happening and good things were on the horizon.

Chapter 16

Melissa sat with her mother while her father and Zach started on the garage repairs. Since the apology letters from the real estate agent and the solicitor made front-page news in the local newspaper, the response to Zach in the town had softened. People who had recently screamed in terror or ordered him out of their business had a change of heart, and while they were not effusive in their welcome, they tolerated his presence with good grace. When she accompanied Zach to the op shop for replacement clothes, Melissa noticed that women gathered in pairs or groups to giggle and simper when she and Zach walked through the business district. The sudden interest of the women in town made her uncomfortable, and while Melissa didn't blame the women, she didn't have to like it.

"Mum, most of the unattached women in town and some of the not-so-available women have noticed that Zach is handsome, and they have started to make overtures to him. Do you think he will put our relationship aside and go out with these women?"

"Lissa, Zach is not a fool. He knows that two weeks ago, the same women called for the police to run him out of town. Even if these women turn his head, he will remember that you trusted him from the start. You offered your friendship when everyone else labelled him a murderer, but you never doubted that there was more to the story. Zach is smart; I don't believe he will overlook you."

"I hope you're right."

The phone interrupted their chat, and she spoke to her dad for the second time today.

"Hi, Liss; how is everything at home?"

"Mum and I are having some girl time, and while we might have to put the spa and massage on the back burner, we are discussing things of worldwide importance."

John Anderson laughed. "Good, let me know when you solve the energy crisis. I've invited Zach for dinner; I hope that is all right. Can you stretch whatever you're preparing for dinner to accommodate one more person?"

"Sure, I can. How long will you guys be?"

" An hour? Will that suit you?"

Melissa fidgeted with the dinner setting, aware that this was Zach's first official meal at their place. She cursed herself for being nervous; it was not as if Zach hadn't eaten with them before, but up until now, it was morning tea and quick lunches. To make this an even more monumental occasion, her mother had asked if she could join them at the table. Melissa prepared some soft foods to accompany her casserole and hoped her mother could eat more tonight than she had at lunchtime.

Once the men arrived, John helped his wife into the wheelchair Zach had made and wheeled her to the table. The conversation centred on the improvements Zach and John intended for the garage. Melissa wondered what Brett did after work most afternoons, and although she feared it was a visit to the pub, she didn't feel that it was her place to interfere. She worried he might regret the many afternoons and evenings he missed sharing with his mother, but Brett would not welcome her interference.

When the phone rang, John left the table and called Melissa a minute or two later.

"It's Doctor Prescott, and I have a terrible feeling that his call will not be good news."

Melissa took the call, and from her end of the conversation, the others could tell that something had gone wrong with the sale of his business. Melissa ended the call and returned to her seat, tears in her eyes.

"Mel, is something wrong?"

Melissa looked at Zach and nodded.

"Mrs Cartwright has offered Doctor Prescott twice as much as we agreed, and she wants him to remain for another six months to train a graduate she is setting up in his practice. It seems James's threat that his mother could make life difficult was accurate. What do I do now?"

The stunned silence at the table didn't bode well for helpful ideas for Melissa. When her mother spoke, it was with anger, and while it heartened Melissa that her mother had the energy and passion to get angry, she worried that the stress might be taxing her strength.

"Damn the woman, and damn that spoiled brat, James. Lissa, your expertise should benefit the community. If we act as a guarantor for a loan, would the bank underwrite a new business? There are vacant shops in the business district that you could modify to house a clinic."

As they considered Pam's suggestion, the thoughts came thick and fast. By the end of the meal, Melissa had the plan to move forward; letting the Cartwrights and their money decide her future was not an option.

When John helped his wife return to her room, Zach and Melissa were alone. Zach wrapped his arms around Melissa, and she rested her head on his chest.

"Mel, if not associating with me will get you what you want, I'd be happy to bow out. I wouldn't be happy, but I'd stop seeing you if that would solve your problem."

Melissa stepped back and looked Zach in the eyes.

"I could stop seeing you, which wouldn't solve the problem. I think James wants to set me up as his mistress and visit me at his leisure. Even if I were happy with that suggestion, it would mean I would never have a family, never have a husband and always be accountable to the

Cartwrights. Why should I stop seeing you when he enjoys the pleasure of his new fiancée?"

"If I didn't know better, I'd think this whole fiasco was fiction from the 1800s. Who has a mistress these days? Aren't they just called "the other woman"? The plan to force you to let James into your bed is bizarre, and it's messing up your life. What are you going to do now?"

"I'll check out some buildings that might be suitable, and then I'll visit the bank manager. But Zach, promise me you won't try to be noble and cut me off. I've grown fond of you, and it would distress me to have you isolate yourself."

Zach stepped closer to Melissa and tangled his fingers in her hair. He used the leverage to pull her closer, and she sighed when his lips met hers. She was far past caring for the man; she feared she was falling for him. The man she had trusted since their first meeting could hurt her if he walked away. Since their first encounter, Melissa's feelings for Zach grew, and her focus on his welfare helped to diminish the hurt James inflicted. The old saying that there is a thin line between love and hate rang true, and James's betrayal obliterated that line, and her hurt feelings morphed into anger and loathing. She wasn't sure if James had the nous to realise his behaviour had pushed her toward Zach, but she was glad he had.

Melissa leaned up and captured Zach's mouth in a sweet kiss. With her parents' needs pushed aside for the minute, Melissa wanted time for herself with Zach. When Zach lifted her in his arms and deposited her on the workbench, Melissa wrapped her legs around his waist and drew him closer. Every time Zach kissed her, he obliterated Melissa's ability to reason, and today was no different.

Chapter 17

"I'm sorry, Melissa, but loaning money for an established business is a far better bet than for a start-up. You can't predict the clientele, and the wages of a receptionist would be a drain from the outset. I want to help, but I can't process your loan application. You might want to look at other options."

"I don't have any other options; Mrs Cartwright has been waving her money around, and every time I find employment, she bribes people to thwart me."

Melissa left the bank; her dreams of making health more accessible in her hometown were now no more than a vision. Her years of hard work and study were for naught unless she left town and started over. There was no way Melissa would turn tail and run; she had too much at stake here in Fleetwood. Her mother was slowly making progress, and Melissa was determined to stay until Doctor Winn assessed her mother's condition. Melissa had to admit to herself that, besides her wish to remain until her mother was well, Melissa didn't want to leave Zach. She wasn't sure how he viewed their fledgling relationship, but Melissa hoped she was more than a temporary diversion.

Melissa drove to the garage with nothing on her schedule for the morning. The exterior work made the place look respectable, and if the interior alterations progress well, Zach should be able to open in about a month. The place was quiet as Melissa walked around the building to the back of the shop. She could hear people talking; the voices belonged to Zach and a woman. Curiosity pushed Melissa forward; she didn't know of any other woman who had befriended Zach. It took her a moment to process the scene in front of her. A woman, bare to the waist, straddled Zach's lap. Heat rushed into her cheeks as she groaned. Zach was seeing other women, and all the while, she foolishly believed they were building a relationship. Zach looked to be struggling with the woman's arms, but Melissa couldn't stand and watch the destruction of her hopes. Zach turned to look at her, anguish in his expression, as Melissa turned and fled. The last time a man had blind-sided her, she finished the afternoon in the pub where she drank too much, and Zach came to her rescue. Today, though, her parents were home, and that's where Melissa was going. She needed her parents' support, and as she drove toward her home, she realised that one of the reasons for staying in Fleetwood was gone. She would have to avoid Zach until her mum was well, and then she'd locate herself in another town where the Cartwrights couldn't bully her, and she didn't have to watch Zach with other women.

Melissa met her father in the hallway as he left her mother's room. The tears that she had kept in check in the car poured from her eyes, and sobs rent her chest. Her dad grabbed her tight, and she remembered the last time someone held her as she cried, making the tears fall even harder. John Anderson steered his daughter from the hallway to the kitchen and sat her in a chair.

"Good heavens, Lissa, what has brought on the waterworks?"

Melissa stuttered through her explanation, watching her father's face tighten. When he sighed and ran his hand through his hair, Melissa felt a pang of guilt. Her father had enough grief without having to deal with her hysterics. He moved to put the kettle on and said, "Let's wait until we have our drinks before we try to sort out your troubles."

When her dad placed the drinks on the table, he pulled up a chair and sat across from Melissa.

"Lissa, I know there are start-up grants for new businesses, but I believe we must admit defeat. Mrs Cartwright's ability to manipulate people through her use of her money is sickening, and I thought better of the people in this town. If you want to leave before we see the results of what Doctor Winn has achieved, I won't stop you. You could find a job in the surrounding areas where Mrs Cartwright has no sway."

"I won't let Mrs Cartwright or Zach drive me away from my home until I see the results of Simon's treatment. But I must admit that I will avoid Zach while I'm here, and then when we get a result, I'll move away. I can't stay in town and watch him with other women. How can he get involved with women who wouldn't give him the time of day a few weeks ago?"

Melissa watched with a frown as her father tipped the remains of his tea into the sink and grabbed his car keys.

"What are you doing?"

"That young man may have broken your heart, but he has also destroyed the friendship we have offered him. I know your mother took a shine to him, and the thought that he could push our friendship aside will hurt her, too. I intend to find out which game he is playing and clarify that he is finishing the repairs to his garage without my help. I'll tell him we don't want anything to do with him."

The door banged behind her father, and Melissa shuffled through the house to her room, where she threw herself on the bed and sobbed. A week ago, she had hoped that things would begin to go smoothly, but it seemed that with every passing day, things got worse. Time passed, and Melissa knew that her mother might need help, and she was wallowing in misery. After washing her face and using a little makeup to repair her face, Melissa headed for her mother's room.

Pam Anderson was dozing when Melissa entered her room. Melissa took her temperature and pulse without speaking, trying not to wake her mother. Using the blood pressure band was sure to wake her mother, and Melissa put it on hold until her mother woke. With her mother asleep, Melissa could scrutinise her face and upper body, which the light sheet didn't cover. Two months into Doctor Winn's treatment, Pam showed signs of weight gain in her face and arms. The sickly yellow colour that she had when Melissa returned from Maccy had disappeared, and her mother had a more normal skin tone. As a health professional, she did not want to get ahead of herself, but the improvements were promising.

Melissa left her mother sleeping and headed to the kitchen to prepare their meal for dinner. But no amount of busy work could remove the ache in her chest and the dread in her stomach. It was ironic that the Cartwrights had tried to destroy her, and regardless of all they had done, it was Zach who dealt the final blow.

Chapter 18

When John pulled up in front of the garage, he drew a deep breath. He was not worried that Zach would threaten him, but he had never interfered in Melissa's personal life before, even when James dumped her. Zach's affection for Melissa showed when they were together, so cheating on her seemed out of character. He would never find answers sitting in the car, second-guessing himself, so he alighted from the vehicle and walked toward the back of the garage. As John walked to the living quarters, such as they were, Zach's anguished gaze zeroed in on him.

"I'm glad to see you are suffering, so maybe you'd better do some explaining. Lissa is devastated, and you caused her grief, so what do you have to say for yourself?"

"I can explain, but dare I say this is Mel's fault and yours as well?"

John Anderson gritted his teeth. "You'd better explain that quickly, or I'll beat you with my bare hands."

"Sit down, John. No one is going to get beaten. When Melissa and I first met, I was a convicted murderer and looked like a homeless man. My hair was well past my shoulders, and my beard hit the middle of my chest. It didn't matter what I looked like because no one would even give me the time of day. And then, this persistent angel got involved in my life, and everything changed. The haircut and shave happened the night before I met you and Pam, thanks to Mel's convincing her uncle to give me a go. Fast forward a few weeks, and you force that cheating pair who sold me this dump to apologise and put it in the paper. Suddenly, I became attractive to women, and they started flirting and throwing themselves at me. I curtailed my trips into town and

91

never responded to their overtures, but some women never give up. I don't even know the name of that chick Mel saw me with. She came in here, and before I could move, she stripped off her shirt and bra and straddled my lap. When Mel saw us, I was trying to dislodge her; by the time I made my disgust in her actions known, I packed her in her car and sent her on her way with a warning for others who might be thinking of trying the same trick. But by then, Mel was long gone."

John watched Zach relate what had happened, but one question bothered him.

"You must have known how distressed Lissa would be after seeing a half-naked woman on your lap; why didn't you follow her home and explain?"

"I care for Mel, and I don't want to lose you guys, but just being with her gives that Cartwright woman an excuse to ruin her life. I was trying to decide if I should let her think I was a cheat to stop her from seeing me, and her problems would stop."

"That woman won't stop until Lissa agrees to be James's mistress. I would suggest she leave town now, but I know she won't leave her mum. Lissa lost the opportunity to open her clinic because the bank wouldn't loan her money for a new business. I'm sure there are start-up loans, but she has conceded defeat. If you care for her, explain what happened and tell her you aren't interested in other women. I'll let you decide, but I suggest you forget about being noble and go and make it right with Lissa."

Zack knocked on the door, his heart in his throat. When the door opened, Zach shoved his foot against the door jam so Mel couldn't close the door. The sight of his face brought on another wave of tears, and Melissa pleaded, "Please, Zach, leave me alone."

What would happen if he couldn't convince her to listen to him? Zach pushed her away from the door and closed it behind himself.

"I will walk away and never bother you again after you hear what I say."

"I thought Dad told you to get lost? "

"Your dad asked for an explanation and accepted my defence. Maybe you should take a leaf out of his book and be open to hearing my explanation."

"Then why couldn't he tell me what you said and save us the trouble?"

"God, Mel, I knew you were stubborn, but I never thought you'd be unreasonable. Why don't you contact me when you can hear without your pride getting in the way?"

Zach turned and headed for the door, but before he could leave, John stopped him.

"I thought you might like to stay for dinner after you and Mel sort out your differences."

"Thanks for the invite, but I won't be staying. Mel won't listen to my explanation; she's too damn proud to accept that there might have been a reason for what she saw, and I refuse to grovel when I did nothing wrong."

Zach extended his hand and shook John's hand.

"Thanks, John. I won't forget your support, but I don't expect you to choose sides."

John swung around to look at his daughter when the door closed behind Zach.

"You told me you care about him, but refuse to listen to his explanation. Your reaction to his request to make things right is unbelievable. I disapprove of your actions, and when another woman snaps him up, you will only have yourself to blame."

Melissa sobbed, "From what I saw, another woman has already snapped him up."

"Things are not always what they seem."

With that cryptic comment, John walked away from his daughter.

Over the next few days, Melissa's misery at missing Zach was made worse by the glares from her father and the sympathetic glances from her mother. On the third morning, Pam waited patiently as Melissa took her vital signs and checked the IV in her hand. Once Melissa had entered the statistics into her patient chart, Pam patted the bed.

"Come and sit with me, Lissa."

Melissa sat on the bed, careful not to jolt her mother.

"Lissa, are you happy? Has ignoring Zach and refusing his explanation given you a sense of peace? Didn't you realise that Zach's explanation to your father had to be believable, or he would have told Zach he wasn't welcome at our house?"

"No, I'm not happy. I miss Zach so much, but I can't think of a possible reason why a bare-breasted woman would be sitting on his lap. No excuse on earth could make that right."

"Lissa, I know Zach feels isolated now that he has lost you, your dad, and me. There is an excuse, a feasible one at that, and you will always wonder what the reason was until you hear what he has to say. Visit him, sit with him, and listen with an open mind. If what he says still doesn't convince you, then walk away with no regrets."

"Why can't you or Dad tell me his reason?"

"Because it's not our story to tell, and if you want a relationship with Zach, be it friendly or romantic, you have to allow him to explain his actions if they upset you."

Melissa sighed. "Okay, I'll visit him when Dad relieves me here."

Chapter 19

Melissa walked to the rear of the garage, her nerves swirling in her stomach, and a sick feeling enveloped her. If Zach wasn't here, she doubted she dared face him another day; it was now or never. Her anxiety escalated when her quarry came into view, and his gaze flitted over her. He then returned to the engine he was servicing.

"Zach, can we talk?"

His cold expression made her cringe. Was he going to make her beg?

"Come back later; I'm busy."

"Um, sure."

Melissa turned to leave; she heard Zach curse and sped up her progress. Just as she reached her car, a large hand grabbed her.

"Damn you, Mel. You pushed yourself into my life, showed me understanding and acceptance, then pulled the rug out from under me, and now you want to talk? Well, fuck you, sweetheart. You make me think I can have a normal life, and then you change your mind. What happens if we sort out this problem and another one surfaces? Would you doubt me at every turn or ask for an explanation? Your mother and father listened and believed me, but the person I care for most threw her hands in the air and refused to talk to me. Why do you want to discuss the issue now?"

Melissa looked at the angry face of the man she had grown to care for and felt her heart lurch. She had caused him as much heartache as he had caused her; now was the time to admit her fault.

"Because I miss you. Mum and Dad won't tell me your reason for what I saw, and I guess I owe you the chance to clear your name. I'm sorry, I wouldn't listen. What I saw shocked and sickened me, and my response was because of the hurt your tryst caused me. Please talk to me, even if you don't have time now. I promise to listen and not judge."

"The car can wait; come inside to discuss what you saw."

As Zach explained, Melissa felt ashamed that her good intentions and her father's had caused the problem Zach now faced. Her face flamed as she remembered climbing into his lap after removing his stitches. Dear God, had she been any better than those women who now found him worthy of their attention? Zach watched her face as a kaleidoscope of emotions washed over her. When Melissa remained silent, Zach rose from his seat, his posture showing defeat. He tried to right the wrong some other woman had caused him, but Mel still didn't believe him.

"Zach, I ..." Melissa's voice caught in her throat.

Zach shrugged. "I can't say anything else to excuse my actions, so there it is."

"Wait, I believe you, but I feel so ashamed. I did the same thing that your unwanted admirer did. I never gave you a choice the day I removed your stitches, and I'm sorry for forcing the issue."

Zach laughed. "I wanted to kiss you the morning you woke up and gave me a blast from your sassy mouth. Every kiss since has been a blessing. Don't lump yourself into the same category as those other women. You weren't afraid of me from the day we met, and you always thought there was more to the story than you had heard. Those women who now want to go slumming by having a fling with me never believed in my honesty and were the same ones who ran screaming from their shops when I entered. You, my sweet, stubborn Mel, are in a class of your own."

"Can I hug you now? Are we done arguing?"

Zach opened his arms, and Melissa stepped into his warm embrace. When he tilted her chin, she gave in to the feeling of his firm lips caressing hers, and Mel thanked her parents for forcing her to hear

Zach's explanation. The bell at the front counter interrupted their private moment, and Zach groaned.

"How the hell am I supposed to build the business when I can't be here fixing cars and welcoming customers out of the front?"

"Well, Mr Mechanic, I am unemployed so that I can be the receptionist. You return to servicing that car, and I'll sort out the customer."

Melissa surveyed the reception area after booking the newest client's vehicle for a service. The whole place needed cleaning and painting, and the furniture's organisation was haphazard; the business could be more functional and welcoming with some reorganisation. Melissa returned to the service bay to ask Zach about cleaning the reception area. With his permission, she rang her dad to discuss possibilities, and they put the cleaning process into place with his assistance.

That night, over dinner, the Andersons and Zach planned the renovation of the old building. The building needed to meet council regulations, so John drew a rough draft of what they needed to change. Not satisfied with a spruce-up, John suggested that the back rooms, which contained a small personal bathroom and an office, be converted into living quarters. They combined the two small toilets, designated for male and female use, to comply with regulations as a disabled unisex toilet. Zach had enough money since the agent and solicitor repaid the extorted money, and a plumber was the first tradesman he would hire. Fired by the change in his circumstances, Zach felt that the business he envisaged while incarcerated might come to fruition.

Hiring some contractors proved problematic as news of the renovation circulated through the town and reached Mrs Cartwight. Tradespeople who had initially quoted for the job were suddenly unavailable, but not deterred, Zach hired contractors from Lonsdale. The price rose once the tradespeople included their travelling costs, but nothing would thwart Zach. Mrs Cartwright might be able to influence the population of Fleetwater, but there were always other tradesmen who welcomed the work.

As the weeks went by, the crumbling shell that Zach bought underwent a complete renovation. Not satisfied with repairing and sprucing the building, John suggested alterations and additions that converted the office area into a small apartment. The final finishing touch was an outdoor area with furniture and a barbecue. Zach surveyed the alterations with awe when the last tradesman packed his equipment and walked away. The transformation of the building from shabby to spruced up was unbelievable. Saving Melissa from herself the night he met her at Trader Jack's was the best thing to happen in his life. Zach doubted he would still be here if he hadn't met her; he would have packed his meagre belongings and moved on. The one thing that caused him guilt was the impact of his relationship on Melissa's life. She hadn't spent four long years studying to become his receptionist. Once the results were in on her mother's illness, would Mel move to a more significant place where she could ply her trade?

Chapter 20

Melissa and Zach settled into a routine, with her acting as his receptionist while he worked on the cars that people suddenly realised could be serviced by someone other than the high-priced dealers in town. Melissa was happy to help out Zach, but couldn't see herself becoming a full-time receptionist after four years of medical training. A notice on the front gate advised clients that the reception area would be unattended from eleven o'clock until one, and this was the time that Melissa sat with he mother, giving John Anderson a well-earned spell. Melissa felt thrilled by the improvement in her mother's condition, and as she became more mobile, Melissa frequently spent time in the garden with he mother.

Once Melissa's two-hour stint with her mother ended, Peggy, the next-door neighbour, called out as she entered the property. After much discussion, John Anderson relented and allowed some of Pam's friends to keep her company, and once they had compiled a roster, he could spend time with friends. John's assistance with the renovation of Zach's garage had pushed the necessity to accept help from others to the forefront.

Melissa called out to Zach as she returned, and after a quick conversation, she pulled the sandwiches from the fridge, and the two retired to the outdoor area. A bell on the driveway would alert them to any cars that pulled up in the driveway, so for a short time, they were alone.

"Mel, what will you do when your mum's treatment ends? As much as I love having you with me, staying here would waste your medical training."

Melissa frowned. "For the time being, I will keep working here, but once I am confident that Doctor Winn's treatment has delivered the required result, I will probably have to move away to get a medical position. I'm unsure whether I'm angrier at James and Mrs Cartwright or the people who let her money persuade them to her way of thinking. The annoying thing is, I heard a rumour that they have had financial difficulties, and even though she spends like there's no tomorrow, her husband is working frantically to shore up their finances. The money she promised the hospital may never materialise, and the money she offered Doctor Prescott might be a pipe dream."

After a moment's silence, Zach said, "If you move, what happens to us?"

Melissa grinned and pulled Zach towards her.

"Don't be thinking for a minute that I'll let you escape. The places I'll be applying to are about an hour or two away, so we can spend some nights together and weekends. I can set up here if Mrs Cartwright isn't forthcoming with the promised funds."

Zach wrapped his arm around Melissa, and she shivered when his lips met hers. How could this man make her lose her ability to think with just one kiss? She hadn't told him she loved him, but if he continued kissing her, Melissa might blurt out how she felt. With a groan, Zach rose.

"I won't finish that ute if I sit here kissing you. Do you want to have dinner somewhere apart from your parents' place tonight?"

"Yeah, I'll tell Dad he has to cook or order takeout."

Melissa scanned the computer and looked for nursing vacancies in the surrounding districts. With her concentration focused on the computer, she didn't hear the vehicle that pulled into the driveway. As it was near closing time, Zach had turned off the alert buzzer, so it surprised Melissa when she realised a car had parked on the driveway's apron. The car's placement annoyed her because an unmistakable message was stencilled on the apron indicating it was a no-standing zone. Melissa closed the computer and pulled the blinds. Three men raced past her to the illegally parked vehicle as she exited the reception area. The driver gunned the engine, and the car tore out of the parking lot, screeching tyres as it hit the roadway and zoomed away. Melissa stood for a moment, attempting to process what she had seen. With dread, she realised something terrible had happened and raced to the service area. Zach had a car on the hoist, but Melissa couldn't see him. She called out to him but dashed towards the apartment when he didn't answer, hoping he had stopped for a toilet break or a drink. Melissa's eyes skimmed over a pile of rags on the floor, and she gave a horrified gasp as her brain registered that what she thought was a pile of rags was Zach's crumpled form. Kneeling beside him, she could see his bloody and battered face; when she found his pulse, it was thready and weak, and even with her medical bag, she doubted she could help. With shaking fingers, she dialled triple zero and gave the operator the address and the urgent need for an ambulance and police officers. She stressed that Zach was in a severe condition and that a rapid response was critical.

When she heard the wail of the ambulance, she raced to the front of the building to direct them to the rear, where Zach lay. Even without a medical degree, she could tell that the blood oozing from Zach's mouth indicated internal injuries. The officers loaded Zach, but the police officers who had just arrived refused to let her accompany him to the hospital. As Melissa watched the ambulance depart, its lights and sirens activated, she felt a wave of nausea.

"Can I call my Dad?"

The officers agreed, and when John Anderson arrived a few minutes later, Melissa collapsed into his arms. John knew something terrible had happened because Melissa was not one for hysterical outbursts. Once he ushered everyone into the flat's lounge area, John made a strong cup of tea for Melissa, and the police officers accepted his offer of coffee.

"I am Constable Barry Tucker, and my colleague is Senior Constable Peter Barnes. Miss Anderson, can you tell us what happened here?"

Melissa recalled the events as she saw them, and the officers asked questions.

What type of car were the men driving?"

"It was a white Toyota Camry; my parents drive the same type of car, so I'm sure that was what it was."

After Melissa described the men as best she could, Peter Barnes said, "I would ask if your boyfriend had any enemies, but considering his reputation, it's a given."

Melissa glared at the officer. "Constable Barnes, the people who don't like him are those who don't read the local newspaper. Once the facts became known, most people accepted his presence in town without trouble."

"If that is the case, why was he attacked so viciously?"

"Because of me."

Officer Tucker crooked an eyebrow. "Would you like to elaborate on that statement?"

Melissa stared at both officers before she said, "It might be better if police from another jurisdiction investigated this assault."

"And why might that be?"

"Officers, this assault is the culmination of a campaign to force me to accept my ex-boyfriend's protection. He and his mother bribed the hospital to fire me. Despite having a contact, she outbid me to take over Doctor Porter's practice, and she ensured the bank wouldn't lend me the money to start a new business. When Zach and my Dad renovated this place, they threatened the local tradies, and we had to get men from further away. If she can influence that many people by waving her money around, I wonder if she can convince you to look the other way on this incident."

The officers looked at each other, and then Constable Tucker said, "So, essentially, you're asking if this wealthy woman can bribe us?"

Melissa blushed, but her answer was firm. "Yes, I guess that's what I'm asking. I'm sorry if that offends you, but recently, I've seen so many people who have followed her demands that I'm sceptical."

Senior Constable Tucker looked from Melissa to John and then replied. "The wealthy woman we are discussing is Mrs Cartwiright; is that correct?"

"Yes."

"She cannot derail the investigation or make us look the other way. If what you say is correct, we may be able to charge her son and her with coercive control. It's a new law, and I'll have to look into it, but that is a start. I'm unsure how to apprehend the men involved because your description is very sketchy."

Melissa was silent for a minute, then said, "If you visit Trader Joe's tonight, the guys shouting at the bar will be the culprits. They'll be the blokes who are generally broke, and tonight they will be flush. Mrs Cartwright must have paid lots for them to risk jail time, and they will be flashing their cash around."

Constable Barnes flipped his notebook shut and grinned.

"Maybe we should hire you, Miss Anderson, to help with our investigations. We'll be in touch."

Melissa slumped in her chair, but her Dad's words revived her.

"I need to get back to your mum; I left her alone because she insisted I help you. I'll see you at the hospital once I find somebody to sit with her. And Lissa, drive carefully. You won't be any help to Zach if you end up in a bed at the same hospital."

Chapter 21

Melissa paced, too anxious to sit as she waited for news about Zach. An hour ago, a nurse informed her that Zach had been taken straight to surgery upon his arrival, but she had heard nothing since then. The door to the waiting room opened, and Melissa turned, hoping it was her father. Much to her surprise, the newcomer was Brett, and when he saw her, he opened his arms, and she fell against him as the tears started again. Once Melissa's tears dried, Brett said, "Do you want a drink? There is a vending machine in the hallway."

When Brett returned, he coaxed Melissa to sit and, taking her hand, said, "He's a strong bloke, Lissa. The waiting is scary, but I bet he'll pull through okay."

Melissa wanted to believe Brett, but seeing Zach's injuries made her less confident than her brother.

"Lissa, I was a doubter when you wanted to start Doctor Winn's treatment on Mum, but I'm glad to say I was wrong. I'm ashamed to admit I didn't help Dad because I couldn't sit by the bed and watch Mum die. Even if we don't get the positive results we want, you have given Dad hope and Mum a better quality of life."

"Thanks for saying that. I didn't want to be bossy or take over, but as I knew what to do, it seemed wrong not to use my medical experience."

Before Melissa or Brett could say anything more, a doctor in scrubs entered the waiting room. Melissa sprang up, and the man said, "Are you the next of kin of Zach Hunter?"

Melissa crossed her fingers behind her back and said, "Yes, I'm his fiancée."

"We operated to remove Mr Hunter's spleen, and there is some damage to his liver, so we had to remove part of it, but the positive thing is the liver will regenerate over time. He has broken ribs; his severe facial injuries include a broken nose and cheekbone. Your fiancé is in the ICU so that you can visit for a moment, but before you do, I must tell you he is in a coma. His head injury is substantial, and we won't know the extent of the damage until he wakes."

The doctor left the room, and Brett put his arm around his sister.

"Fiance, eh?"

"He doesn't have any next of kin worth a damn, and I didn't know if the doctor would let me see Zach if I said I was his girlfriend. Come with me, please?"

Brett nodded. He didn't know how bad Zach looked; nurse or not, he wouldn't let Lissa face her injured boyfriend alone.

Melissa entered the room first, and Brett knew Zach's appearance must be dire by his sister's strangled cry. When he cleared the door, he saw why Melissa was distressed. Zach had a breathing tube inserted, and from the damage to his face, Brett doubted that the bloke could breathe without it. A bandage covered the top of his head, and the sheet pulled to his waist revealed the stitches that closed the incisions the surgeons had made. A bevy of tubes protruded from his body, and Brett's earlier declaration that Zach would recover tasted like ash in his mouth. A nurse evicted them only moments after they entered Zach's room, assuring Melissa she could return the following day.

For the next three days, Melissa juggled her mother's treatment with visits to Zach. Some days, Brett accompanied Melissa; others, her father kept her company. Still, the anguish of keeping watch over her comatose boyfriend could not diminish, regardless of who kept her company. As she sat holding his hand, she prayed for his recovery. Melissa rested her head on the bed next to Zach's face, but she raised her eyes when she saw a man and a woman walk into the room. The realisation of who the people were shot through Melissa, and her blood boiled.

The man glared at her. "Who are you?"

"I'm Melissa, and I'm Zach's fiancée. I know who you are, and I have to say Zach would want neither of you here pretending to care."

The woman spoke. "If you know who we are, surely you can allow us time with Zach."

"I will leave you alone for now, but when you have finished visiting, we need to talk."

Melissa bent forward and kissed Zach before exiting the room.

Half an hour later, Michael and Mrs Hunter left Zach's room and met her in the waiting room, without preamble. Michael verbally attacked Melissa.

"I don't believe that hogwash about you being his fiancée; he would have let us know if he was engaged. You're some prison groupie that Zach picked up along the way. Why would you bother hanging around now that he's injured? Are you hoping to score big if he dies? What was the interest in taking up with a con? Were you going to brag to your other slutty friends that you slept with a murderer? You're nothing but an opportunistic whore that Zach was too stupid to send packing."

Melissa looked at the man, Zach's brother, and understood that his ego and self-interest were his top priorities. Promising not to lose her temper, Melissa shook her head.

"Why would Zach tell you if he was engaged? Aren't you the brother who cleared out when you turned eighteen and left Zach to cope with seeing his mother beaten up daily? And I'm sure I'm not mistaken, aren't you the bloke who never stood up for your brother when he saved your mother's life? You never visited him in jail and banished him to another town so he wouldn't ruin your reputation. You lied and told him you saw the property he wanted to buy. He's been living in third-world conditions, starving because the agent and solicitor perpetrated a lie that made the entire community turn against him. You, Michael, are a sorry excuse for a brother."

As Michael blustered, Melissa turned to the woman standing next to Michael.

"When a woman is too afraid to leave her abusive husband, that's a tragedy, but a woman who places her children in danger is a disgrace. When your husband beat Zach, and you had to go to the hospital, the workers tried to convince you to leave your husband, but you refused. You said his violence and alcohol were due to frustration at work, and he needed your support. He didn't need help; he needed a punching bag, and you subjected your sons to that violence every day. The man you loved died when the alcohol and violence were born, and you were too stupid to realise. If Zach hadn't arrived when he did, you would be dead, but did you stand up for him in court? Did you go to visit him in jail? Have you ever said thank you? The day Zach told me of his history, he said that if he ever decided to ask his family for help, I should remind him why it would be a bad idea. He wouldn't want you here, so now that you've done your duty, you should return to your perfect lives and leave the people who love Zach to help him."

Chapter 22

Melissa ran the stats on her mother and filled in her chart. She took a photo of her mother in bed, and when she went into the kitchen to eat breakfast, Melissa took more pictures. The charts showing her mother's stats during the trial were essential. They had been using Doctor Winn's medication for a few weeks before it occurred to her to take photos so that the improvement in her mother's condition could be visible to any doubters.

"What do you want to do today, Mum?"

"Do you think I could accompany you when you visit Zach?"

"I'm not sure that the hospital would allow you to visit. I only get to see Zach because I said I was his fiancée, and now that his mother and brother are here, I think that might be the limit. What about I go by myself today, and I'll speak to the head nurse?"

"If visiting Zach is off the menu, I thought I might do some baking. I can sit in the chair Zach made for me, and if I get tired, I'll have a lie-down."

"What are you doing today, Dad? "

"While Peggy is here, I thought I might spend the morning at the men's shed. The guys were such a help fixing Zach's garage that I'd like to offer my time to help with the toy drive they have organised."

"It seems like everyone has organised their day. I'm going into the hospital, and I hope that arrogant brother and neglectful woman feel like they've done their duty and leave town."

As Melissa entered the hospital, she wondered what working here would have been like. The number of patients and the seriousness of the injuries seemed less than at Maccy, but she regretted that Mrs

Cartwright had so much influence in the town. She felt compelled to find the man who sacked her to uncover the source of the funds for the new wing. Would they offer her a job when it became apparent that the promised funds were not forthcoming?

Melissa pushed through the doors to the ICU when a security guard stepped in front of her.

"Where are you going, Miss?"

"Why are you asking? Is there a problem?"

Melissa's blood froze. Dear God, Zach couldn't have died during the night, could he?

"I'm visiting my fiancé, Zach Hunter."

"Mr Hunter's brother and mother are here now, and they've requested that we not allow anyone who is not family to visit."

"Why would they stop me from visiting? I'm his fiancée; surely I have a right to see Zach?"

"Mr Zach Hunter had his brother listed as next of kin in the papers found in his wallet, and as next of kin, Mr Michael has the right to make decisions if necessary. I'm sorry, miss, but he was clear on not allowing others to visit Mr Hunter."

Melissa drove home in a daze. How could Michael stop her from visiting Zach? She would tackle him if she knew where he and his mother were staying, but the town had too many options for visitors to use as temporary accommodation. Was this action a response to what she said yesterday? When Melissa arrived home, her mum and Peggy were in the kitchen, chatting and cooking. Pam Anderson looked at her daughter's face and knew something was wrong.

"Sit here, Lissa and tell me what is wrong."

As Melissa told her mother what had happened at the hospital, her mother's shocked expression reflected Melissa's.

"I don't know if he's awake or still in a coma. What can I do?"

"Why don't you ring the hospital and ask how he is? I know it's not as good as seeing him, but at least you can keep abreast of his condition," said Peggy.

"Yes, Lissa, that's a good idea. Do that now."

Melissa scrolled through her contacts and selected the hospital's phone number. She requested an update on Zach's condition, and the woman who answered the phone put her on hold. While listening to elevator music, Melissa wondered why she had to wait. Couldn't they look at their patient records and answer her question?

"Hello, this is Nurse Jennings from the ICU. I believe you were asking for an update on Zach Hunter?'

"Yes. Even though I'm Zach's fiancé, his brother and mother have restricted visitors to family only."

"I'm very sorry, Miss Anderson, but Mr Michael Hunter has asked that we not reveal any information regarding his brother's condition in the interests of privacy."

"Please, don't I have the right to know how he is?"

"I'm sorry, Miss Anderson, my hands are tied."

Melissa's anger after James's surprise engagement party was minor compared to her hatred for Michael. Melissa had managed to keep her spirits up, even when Mrs Cartwright thought of a new and painful way to thwart her plans, but the pain of Michael's vengeful actions caused indescribable anguish. How could she go about her daily activities if she couldn't be at the hospital to support Zach?

Pam and John Anderson watched with concern as Melissa struggled to get through her days. With Zach's garage closed, she didn't have a job, and the hours of the day dragged for her. Each morning, after tending to her mother, Melissa drove to the hospital and sat in the waiting room. It angered her when she realised that Michael and his mother visited for less than an hour once a day; what could it hurt to let her see Zach? The thought of sneaking into the ICU crossed Melissa's mind, but the ever-vigilant security guard put paid to that idea.

Seven days after Zach's attack, Melissa entered the hospital to be greeted by the security guard.

"Miss Anderson, your daily vigil needs to end. The Hunter family left town last night. Mr Michael Hunter transferred his brother to another hospital closer to his home."

"Which hospital did he transfer Zack to?"

The guard gave a sympathetic grimace. "I'm sorry, I'm not at liberty to say."

When Melissa returned home and divulged the latest cruel jab Michael had inflicted on her, her parents were at a loss to find a way to help their daughter. After a night of self-absorbed misery and tears, Melissa buckled down to help her mother regain the muscle tone in her legs. Physio exercises were not Melissa's specialty, but the local physio set up a plan for her to follow, giving her something to focus on instead of her misery. At night, Melissa sat with her laptop on her knee, searching for nursing positions that fit her criteria. She wanted to be close to her family but away from the poison of the Cartwright family.

Three weeks after Zach's hospital transfer, John Anderson requested that Melissa and her brothers be present at the evening meal. The request surprised Melissa, but since she had nowhere else to go, it was probably more for Brett than her. Dinner passed off without her parents clarifying their reason, and when they carried away the plates and dispersed the tea and coffee, John Anderson cleared his throat.

"Lissa, even without the final scan on your mother, you have given us a second chance, and we intend to make the most of it. If the scan is clear, or the tumours are small enough to be operable, we want to make the most of the time left. It never occurred to me that the small town of Fleetwood would be a toxic place to raise our family, and because of what has happened here, we are moving away."

"I don't blame you; I've looked at nursing vacancies across the state, but I wanted to stay close to you and Brett. If you choose a location, I will see if anything is close."

"Maybe we could do it another way. Your Dad and I are going travelling when I get my diagnosis. We won't buy a caravan, but we can see a lot of Australia even if we stay at motels and caravan parks, and when we finish, we could move close to wherever you settle."

"Okay, Brett, what's your take on this?"

Brett looked at his family and cleared his throat.

"I've wanted to talk to you about my plans, but I've put it off with everything that's happened here."

"Well, big brother, fill us in."

"I will finish my apprenticeship in two months and want to leave Fleetwood. I have a friend who lives in Prescott, and he has contacts with people who will interview me for a job."

"Why haven't we heard of this friend before?" Melissa asked.

Brett blushed bright red and looked down as he said, "Actually, he's my partner. I'm gay."

The laughter that followed Brett's announcement seemed unworthy of her parents, and Melissa glared at them. Before she could take her parents to task, her Dad said, "Sorry, son. Your mother and I are not laughing at your announcement, but at the time it took you to officially inform us. We've known for years that you are gay; I guess it took a while to come to terms with your sexuality."

Melissa and Brett looked at each other and started to laugh.

"Here I was thinking I was discreet, and you guessed?"

Pam nodded. "Think about your school years. You played male-only team games and hung out with friends at the pub. When girls came on the scene, and your mates struggled to talk to the girls or impress them, you had no difficulty because you felt no attraction. Sure, you took a girl to the prom, but she was a friend, not a date. When can we meet your partner?"

"You want to meet him?"

"Is he a passing fancy or a serious partner?"

His father's question surprised Brett.

"It's serious."

"Then, son, we want to meet this man who may become part of our family."

With the agreement on leaving Fleetwood, the discussion turned to possible relocation locations. Brett's partner, Daniel, lived in Prescott, a small community half an hour outside Lonsdale. The thought of coming across Zach or his horrid family in Lonsdale dimmed Melissa's enthusiasm for the small community. There was no urgency in deciding where to go because they had to finalise her mother's treatment. After the next two weeks, Dr Winn would conduct a full-body scan of Pam, and then they would plan a course of action. Melissa collated the weekly charts and placed the photos of her mother taken during her treatment in a scrapbook. After discussions with her parents and Simon Winn, they agreed they would go to the national broadcaster if the treatment were successful. The result appeared optimistic with Pam's weight gain and healthy demeanour.

The family was on tenterhooks, waiting for Simon to arrive with the images from the scans and the X-ray negatives. When Simon walked into the room with a grin, tears of joy and squeals of excitement filled the room. The one sobering thing was a slight abnormality in Pam's uterus, so they would schedule a hysterectomy in the next few days. Melissa thanked God for sparing her mother and knew that after the surgery, the family owed it to the world to make the medical fraternity acknowledge the effectiveness of the treatment Simon developed. Once the medicine's history became public, thousands of people were willing to test the product. All the terrible things that had happened since James's engagement party faded into insignificance when she considered the joy of her mother's recovery.

Chapter 23

Melissa checked the readout on her ringing phone. She wasn't sure whether to feel happy or sad as she answered the phone. Barry Tucker greeted her when Melissa answered, and she said, "Do you have good news for me?"

"Melissa, I have great news for you. The three thugs who assaulted your boyfriend pleaded guilty and accused Mrs Cartwright of paying them to beat up Zach Hunter. Your ex didn't want to be the only one charged with coercion, so he dobbed his mother in, too. I've never come across so many criminals willing to accuse each other. We won't need a trial since everyone except Mrs Cartwright confessed, and after the accusations against her, no amount of high-class barristers will get her off."

"Gosh, that is great."

"Another thing that might make you smile is that your ex was to marry the other woman to shore up the Cartwrights' finances, which need help."

"That's karma for those who threw me over for recognition from that woman. The hospital is short of a nurse practitioner, Doctor Prescott won't be able to retire, and all those tradies who wouldn't work for Zach have lost out. It serves them right. Thanks for telling me, Barry and thank Peter, too."

Melissa ended the call, and although the news Barry Tucker had relayed was welcome, it didn't remove the hurt the Cartwrights had inflicted. With a sigh, Melissa focused on the business at hand and called through the next patient. After much hunting, Melissa discovered a clinic that a doctor was setting up in Prescott. The clinic was in its infancy, but the doctor, Steven Wright, envisioned it becoming a one-stop shop for medical treatment in the district. Arriving at the clinic at its inception was fortunate for Melissa, as she was able to set her own hours and begin building her own patient list. Melissa had looked for hospital vacancies, but after her treatment at Fleetwood Hospital, she realised that small community hospitals would sell their souls for extra funding. She didn't want to be a pawn in the political games hospitals played, so the clinic was a refreshing change.

The fly in the ointment was Prescott's proximity to Lonsdale. The larger town had more services than the smaller community, and Melissa was always on edge when she ventured into the city. Even though six months had passed, she feared running into any of the Hunter family. Her move away from Fleetwood was seamless. Her parents sold their house quickly and, after her mother's surgery, headed off into the unknown. Melissa had moved in with Daniel, Brett's partner. The two got along well, but Melissa was aware that within months, Brett would move to Prescott to be with his partner, and when that happened, Melissa had no intention of being the third wheel. The small cottage that Melissa discovered on the real estate website suited her perfectly. It was an old miner's cottage that the previous owners had refurbished, and although it was small, Melissa had no need for numerous bedrooms and bathrooms.

After the National broadcaster aired the documentary on Dr Winn's breakthrough, Melissa's parents left the cities because their participation in the program compromised their privacy. Their end date was unconfirmed, and their destination was wherever the urge took them. Melissa envied her parents' ability to take a day at a time but knew in her heart that, eventually, they would return to the area to settle near their children. It pleased Melissa that her parents had taken this second chance at life, and when she talked to them, they sounded upbeat and happy.

As the workload at the clinic increased, Melissa had less and less time to remember the disappointments and heartbreak that she had left behind in Fleetwood. At night, she opted for takeout or frozen dinners because it hardly seemed worth the effort of cooking a meal for one. Melissa's one home-cooked weekly meal was Sunday lunch when she joined Brett and Daniel. The Sunday lunches were fun and casual, and it pleased Melissa to see how happy her brother was. After her brother came out, her parents' memories of Brett's childhood and young adolescence triggered her memories of her brother's past. She, too, would have realised what her brother was hiding had she not been so focused on her studies and her busy life. While Melissa lived with Daniel, she discovered he was a good cook. Even though she knew she had to have her own living space, she missed his cooking, so Sundays were a highlight of the week.

"Lissa, when do you think our parents will return?"

"I'm not sure. Mum and Dad are having such a good time that they may become permanent grey nomads. Honestly, after what they went through with cancer, I don't blame them for making the most of this second chance. They had to become the face of the documentary that the national broadcaster produced about Simon's treatment, but it robbed them of their privacy. I know Dad changed their phone numbers, and he and Mum closed their online portals because there was a lot of interest in the treatment and trolls who criticised them for being selfish."

David shook his head. "I can't understand why your parents received any criticism. The people who should be in the firing line are the selfish medical practitioners who wouldn't allow Simon access to their patients for a trial. Imagine how angry and devastated you would feel if a loved one died of cancer while this drug reclined in fridges in Simon's lab."

Brett agreed. "You're right, and I thank God Lissa worked with Simon and knew of the success of the drug. I'm not sure, Lissa, if I ever said sorry for being a doubting Thomas and thank you for all you did. You were right when you criticised me for not helping Dad, but I couldn't sit with Mum daily and watch her getting weaker and weaker."

"It was easier for me because I came in at the end of that torturous period, but my medical training helps."

Brett's next question stunned Melissa.

"Do you regret getting involved with Zach? Mum and Dad loved him, and his actions gutted us all, but it had to be worse for you. Do you still miss him?"

Melissa closed her eyes, and instantly, the handsome face of the man she fell in love with materialised. With a sigh, she tried to organise her thoughts.

"Do I regret getting involved? The answer is no. My life would have been worse if he hadn't saved me the night I went to Trader Joe's. Even though Mrs Cartwright eventually tried to use Zach to push me into a relationship with James, she would have done the other things even if he wasn't on the scene. I miss him every day in so many ways that the only way to survive the heartache is to work until I drop. It has to get easier, but I will always regret how it ended and hate Michael Hunter and Mrs Hunter."

Chapter 24

S ix months later

John and Pam walked towards the coffee shop. Their morning ritual was to try a new eatery in the Lonsdale area. Today, they chose a café called Susie's Treats because they had heard good things about it. The drive from their new home in Prescott did not inhibit their enthusiasm for trying new things. A male voice called out as John steered them around a group of people blocking the footpath. Turning to see who had hailed her, Pam saw Zach Hunter's smiling face. Forgetting the anger and hurt he inflicted, Pam reached out and hugged Zach.

"You look terrific, Pam. I saw the documentary, and it was great, although I know you came under a lot of criticism for using the treatment when so many people could have benefited. But rational people would know that the drug's restriction wasn't your fault."

Pam ran her eyes across Zach's face and body and said, "You look good, too. How long were you in the hospital?"

John's voice interrupted the conversation.

"I find it extraordinary that you can greet Pam like an old friend after what you did to us. After welcoming you into our family, you pushed us away, breaking Lissa's heart. I'm pleased you are well, but I don't believe I have anything to say to you, and it surprises me that Pam can talk to you despite the hurt you caused our family."

Zach frowned. "This conversation makes no sense. I didn't push you all away; my brother told me you were worried about Mel's safety and didn't want anything to do with me."

Pam squeezed his arm. "Here on the footpath is not the place to air our dirty laundry. We live in Prescott now; why don't you call around after you finish work?"

Zach nodded, and after exchanging details, they parted.

Zach pulled up outside a ranch-style house set on a large block. The house was as unlike the place in Fleetwood as it could get, but Zach could see the property's appeal. Zach rubbed his sweaty palms on his jeans as he alighted from the car. He had come straight from work, and as jeans and a company shirt were what he wore each day, Zach figured the Andersons would have to accept his attire. Although Zach walked towards the front door, he questioned his decision to come here. When they met outside the coffee shop, John Anderson was angry, and Zach didn't want an acrimonious exchange with people he once revered.

The front door opened before Zach could change his mind and leave. Pam smiled, although her smile was more constrained than it had been in town.

"Come through to the kitchen, Zach. I always think that facing each other when discussing an issue is better. Have a seat, and I'll make coffee. Do you still drink it black?"

Zach shook his head. "I only ever drank it black because I never had a way to keep milk cold, but now I live in a home I can splurge."

Once everyone had a drink before them, Zach said, "Maybe you should start this conversation because the things you said in the street made no sense to me."

John nodded. "I could go right back to the start, but we all know how we got to the end. The day of the assault, Mel rang me; she was almost hysterical, and while I had trouble understanding what had happened, I knew she needed support. Pam urged me to go, saying she would be fine. When I arrived at the garage, ambulance officers were loading you into an ambulance. As they hit the lights and sirens as they reached the road, I knew you were in serious trouble. The police officers questioned Lissa, and I was concerned that Mrs Cartwright's influence might extend to the police force, but it turned out that it did not. Once the police finished, I returned home to see if I could find someone to sit with Pam and Lissa went to the hospital. When Brett arrived home, he offered to wait with his sister at the hospital. Lissa told the staff she was your fiancée because she didn't think they would let her in if she were your girlfriend."

"Ah, that makes sense. I couldn't determine why Michael cursed my fiancé, but now I understand."

Pam took over the narrative. "After your assault, Melissa spent a few hours with me each day doing the exercises the physio prescribed and then went to the hospital to sit with you."

Zach interrupted. "Why would she do that? When my mother and brother arrived, she told them she was done with me because it was too dangerous to associate with me. She told Michael that the relationship with me was a fling, and she never intended it to go further."

John shook his head. "Do you remember after we fixed your legal mess from purchasing the garage? You asked if you ever considered asking your family for help to remind you why it was a bad idea."

"Ah, yeah, sure. Why is that relevant?"

"Your brother is a self-centred, egotistical pig, and what he said about Melissa was not true."

Pam, who had listened quietly as her husband spoke, finally said, "Zach, Lissa sat next to your bed for three days, and when your brother arrived, he and Lissa argued. He called Lissa a prison whore and suggested that she prostituted herself to brag to other whores that she slept with you. He said other things in the same vein, and Lissa lost her temper and told him that he was a lousy brother, and your mother was a selfish, neglectful mother."

Zach looked sick at the revelations of John and Pam.

"What happened then?"

Pam reached out and placed her hand on Zach's arm.

"Because you had him listed as your next of kin, Michael got to call the shots. He instructed the hospital staff that only family could visit and prohibited them from telling callers how you were under the guise of privacy protection. Michael shut Lissa out, and despite her daily visits to try to change his mind, he refused. The day they transferred you, Lissa first found out when the security guard told her she was wasting her time because you weren't there.

Zach looked dazed. "I asked to see Mel almost every day, and Michael kept saying she didn't want to see me, and she asked him to tell me that our friendship was over. He said Mel told him she wouldn't be in a relationship with an ex-con."

John left the room and returned with a bottle of whisky. He poured them all a generous portion, and once they put their glasses on the table, he said,

"Considering her support before she knew about your history, didn't that seem a bit disingenuous?"

" I guess I never thought about it too much. Her supposed abandonment of me hurt so badly that I tried to block it from my mind. What happens now?"

"That's up to you."

"I need to see Mel, and you might have to give me her address because we all know if I ring her, she will block my call. The visit will have to wait until tomorrow because I am too angry to be rational. I'm going home to pack my bags, and even if I have to stay in a motel for a week, I will find my place. Michael and my mother have never shown the slightest care for my feelings, and Michael was more concerned with getting revenge on Mel for telling the truth than with my welfare. I will cut them out of my life; they are dead to me."

After Zach left, John and Pam sat together on the couch. "All that hurt and anguish because that egotist had to seek revenge on Lissa for speaking the truth. Is it possible for us to sort this mess?"

Pam nodded. "Yes, Zach and Lissa will be together once she hears his explanation."

Chapter 25

When Zach left the Andersons' home, he was furious. The numerous times Michael had disappointed him were too many to count. How had Michael grown into a man who placed his family's welfare much lower than his wishes? Was that a response to seeing his mother put them all in jeopardy? Was it a response to seeing his father a broken man after the company retrenched? There were no answers to Zach's questions. He remembered his brother's ambition to own a business. When had his ambitions blocked out his humanity? Before Michael abandoned him when the police arrested him, numerous incidents of his brother's self-serving behaviour swirled through his mind. Not only did Michael's behaviour infuriate Zach, but the fact that his mother did nothing to rectify Zach's belief that the Andersons had abandoned him made him angry.

Pulling his car into the driveway of the house he shared with his brother and mother, Zach stalked up the footpath to the front door. He decided to pack his bags before speaking to his family because if he lost his cool and stormed out of the house, he would have to return later to collect his belongings. With a case open on his bed, Zach emptied the clothes from the drawers and cupboards. He grabbed things and stuffed them into the suitcase, and he knew later he would regret not folding his belongings, but he didn't have the patience required.

Zach left his packed suitcase by the front door and walked towards the kitchen, where he could hear his brother and mother's voices. His mother smiled at him as he entered the room, and he wondered how the woman could look at herself in the mirror. Did she ever remember the events of the past with regret? The lack of a returning smile warned

Mrs Hunter that Zach was unhappy. Zach shook his head in exasperation. His mother's selfishness had ruined his life; even now, she was taking the easy way out and not calling Michael on his lies.

"Bad day, bro?"

"Yes, but enlightening at the same time. You'd never guess who I ran into today?"

Michael caught the menace in Zach's question, but shrugged as if the answer was of no concern.

"No? No guesses? I'll tell you, shall I? I ran into John and Pam Anderson. I've just returned from their home, where they explained what happened when I was in the hospital. Why Michael? Why punish me further? Didn't you do enough by abandoning me during the arrest and trial? Didn't you cause me enough distress by telling me the garage was a good buy? What have I done to you to make you hate me so much?"

Michael placed both hands on the table and glared at Zach.

"You, little brother, were always a millstone around my neck when we were kids, and now you've become an impediment to expanding my business. People find it hard to trust a man if his brother is an ex-con. Besides, that bitch shot off her mouth, so I paid her back by refusing to let her visit you."

"Why did you need to pay her back? Was it that everything she said was true, and you had no reasonable excuse for your treatment of me? I'm not sure why I was a millstone; I was just a kid trying to survive the shit show that was our home life. Did it ever occur to you that without my intervention, our mother would be dead or a vegetable in a hospital, further draining your precious reserves?"

"I don't have to listen to this shit."

"Why? Is it too hard to listen to the unembellished truth? Even after you lied about the condition of the garage, you couldn't even offer an apology. I lived in third-world conditions, with furniture looted from the dump, and you never bothered to check on me. You won't have to worry; I am packed and ready to leave, but first, I must ask Mum why you let Michael lie to me?"

Zach watched as his mother wrung her hands, and then a look of determination crossed her face.

"That girl was the reason those men assaulted you. Why should we let the girl who caused your injuries off without punishment?"

Zach laughed hysterically. When he got himself under control, he said. "Your husband beat you daily, but he never faced the consequences because you were delusional. When Dad hit me, and the hospital workers tried to convince you to leave him, you refused. The police never charged him for beating me because you declined to press charges. When the social workers at the hospital tried to convince you to leave Dad, you refused.

The man you loved died when the company he worked for retrenched him; you were too stupid to see that. After he beat me, you took me home, where I wasn't safe because you were too pathetic to consider the safety of your children and leave. You have never protected me, but I hoped you would do the right thing by me when Michael's lies estranged me from a family who cared for me. Without that family, I would have starved to death or thrown a rope over the roof trusses and hung myself. The Anderson family showed me what family life should look like, as if I needed the truth that our family life was toxic. You needn't worry; this is my last interaction with you two. You are dead to me, so don't try to contact me again. No apologies or regrets will ever be enough."

Zach walked away from his mother and brother without a backward glance. The toxic relationship was over, and he looked forward to reuniting with Mel and building a relationship with her family. He just hoped that what Michael did to Mel wouldn't be irreparable.

Epilogue

Zach followed John's directions to Mel's tiny cottage, his nerves far worse than they had been the night before facing Pam and John. Meeting Mel and getting her to listen was a tough ask, especially as he hadn't seen her in more than six months, but after dealing with his family, he was eager to move on. The night before had been ugly; his brother took no blame for lying to him, and his mother took the easy way out, refusing to take responsibility for her part in the lies. His mother was a weak-willed woman who always took the easy way out, even if it meant his father beating her every night. Michael was a pompous, arrogant ass, and his focus was always on what was best for Michael. He had cut them from his life and would be better for it.

When Zach pulled up outside the cottage that was Mel's home, he was determined to explain what had happened and seek her forgiveness. The house was quiet, and there was no response when he knocked on the door. Mel's car was in the driveway; had she seen him approach and refused to answer the door? Zach banged on the door, and this time, someone inside the house responded. The sound of the locks disengaging gave Zach hope that Mel might answer the door without checking who her visitor was.

Melissa flung the door open and came face-to-face with Zach. Her wet hair and hastily donned clothes suggested that Melissa was in the bath before his interruption. Melissa looked shocked when she saw her visitor, and as she moved to shove the door closed, Zach stuck his foot in the doorway, blocking it.

"Oh, no, you don't. We need to talk, and slamming the door in my face isn't conducive to conversation. Let me in, Mel."

"Go away, Zach, you've caused me enough grief. If you don't leave, I'll call the police."

"And will you tell them your parents gave me your address?"

Melissa was stunned by this revelation and, against her better judgment, stepped back from the door and let Zach enter. He may have entered her house, but Melissa had no intention of making him welcome.

"You have ten minutes to say whatever brought you here, and then you must leave."

Zach hooked her hand through his arm and said, "Where's the kitchen?"

"Why do you want the kitchen? Don't be thinking I'm going to make you a drink."

"Yesterday, your mum said it is easier to face someone when discussing a problem, and I agree."

"You were at my parents' house yesterday?"

"Yes. Please, Mel, let's sit down, and I can tell you what brought me here.

Reluctantly, Melissa sat at the kitchen table facing Zach.

"I should start with how I ended up in your parents' house, and then I'll explain my reason for visiting."

Zach recounted his chance meeting with Melissa's parents and the reason for the ensuing discussion, and Melissa listened, unsure where this was going.

"Your parents and I had a different take on what happened when I was in the hospital, and my argument with Michael and my mother last night validates what your father said."

Zach explained the events her father outlined, and when he put his understanding on the table, Melissa could see that Michael had duped them all.

"What did he hope to gain by alienating us?"

"I think when you argued with him, and everything you said rang true, he decided to get revenge."

Melissa rose from the table and turned on the kettle.

"Do you still drink it black?"

Zach laughed. "Your Mum asked me the same question, and the answer is no; I don't drink it black. I drank it black when I lived in the garage because I couldn't keep the milk cold, and it went off before I could use it."

Melissa shook her head.

"God, you lived in third-world conditions, and the first morning when I woke up, I couldn't believe the squalor. I bought you breakfast to thank you for saving me, but it looked like you hadn't had a decent meal in a while, and I was scared you'd starve to death."

"I might have taken the easy way out and ended it if you hadn't blundered into my world. Nothing in my life convinced me I was worthwhile until you entered my life. I saved you that night at the pub because I couldn't see any alternative, and when you came to get your tyre fixed, I was concerned that you would upset my solitary existence. I knew I could not keep you away when you treated me at the hospital, but the more I saw, the more I congratulated myself for that first rescue."

Melissa laid the coffee cup in front of Zach and took her seat.

"What happens now?"

Zach felt he needed to express what he wanted from Mel, hoping she would feel the same.

"We can't ignore the shit my family put us through, but Mrs Cartwright is no longer messing with our lives. I want a lasting relationship with you, so if you're not in it for the long run, we say no hard feelings and walk away."

"I'm finding it hard to reconcile what we shared before to a new life. You sold the garage; what are you doing for a job?"

"I work at Parker's as a stock and land agent."

Melissa laughed. "What do you know about stock?"

Zach smiled. "Parkers were willing to train me, and I decided I needed more skills than I could get as a washed-up mechanic. Mel, please, let me back into your life. I miss you so much. We can take our time to build a relationship; without interference, we can repair the damage Michael and the Cartwrights did."

Melissa locked her fingers in Zach's as she spoke.

"When you sat beside me at the pub, I felt safe. Something about you resonated with my soul, and it never occurred to me to be afraid of you. I trusted you, and you never broke that trust. What we had together gave me the strength to battle fate's hand, and then you were gone. God, Zach, you can't know how scared and angry I was. I knew what happened at the hospital resulted from my argument with Michael, and I could have kicked myself for telling him what I thought of him and your mum. Every day, until Michael transferred you, I sat in the waiting room hoping to change his mind, and every day, he and your mum ducked out the back way or never even visited. I was so angry; I didn't know if you were still in a coma, and the hospital couldn't tell me anything because your family forbade any information from being shared with others to protect your privacy. I hoped you would call me when you were better, but when I heard nothing, I had to conclude that you had a hand in cutting me off."

"Mel, I'm so sorry. What Michael said about you never rang true, but I had to believe him when you never visited. If it helps, I was in anguish thinking you had finished with me."

Melissa closed the distance between them and touched Zach's chest. "I don't want what we had; I want more and better. I want you in my life, my family and my future with no outside interference and no hateful people causing us grief."

Zach wrapped his arms around Melissa. "Thank God; I want the same things, Mel. I want a life with you, and that means marriage and kids. Please don't panic; we have time to get to those things, but I want to spend as much time as possible with you. Are you up for that?"

"Yes, I want those things too, but let's take time to date and reconnect. When we were together, we went out only twice: once to the diner and once to the Chinese restaurant. I want dinners, trips to tourist spots, and quiet nights on the couch watching tellie. Are you up for that?"

Zach laughed when she used his words, but he was up for anything Melissa suggested as long as they could be together.

Don't miss out!

Visit the website below and you can sign up to receive emails whenever Robyn C Rye publishes a new book. There's no charge and no obligation.

https://books2read.com/r/B-A-FKBW-WYDFC

Also by Robyn C Rye

Farnsworth Sisters
Marrying a Rogue
Rescuing Hannah

The Buckingham Sisters
Lady Maggie's Challenge
Layla's Unwanted Husband

The Evans Family
Sometimes Love is not Enough
Still the One
Moving Forward

Standalone
One More Chance
Lady Jayne's Reputation
Third Time's the Charm
Can't Stop Loving You

The Marriage Scam
An Unlikely Match
Searching For You
The Unexpected Suitor
The Lady and the Duke
Starting Over
An Unforgettable Stranger
The Duke's Revenge
The Temporary Wife
Against The Odds
Betrayed
No Good Turn Goes Unpunished
Lady Eloise's Soldier
Lillian's Forbidden Beau
Remember Me
Always Second Best
When One Door Closes
Coming Home to You
Chasing Shadows
Fool Me Once
Deserting Lady Audrey
My Unlikely Saviour
Lies and Deception
A New Beginning
Julia's Second Chance
The Hidden Enemy
The Maiden's Redemption
Miss Elizabeth's Season

www.ingramcontent.com/pod-product-compliance
Lightning Source LLC
Chambersburg PA
CBHW021215130726
47988CB00002B/663